Without warning ... head high and trying to rear.

"What the..."

A hollow, booming report sounded only a few yards distant, followed immediately by the wet, ugly slap of lead striking flesh and bone. The horse became dead weight between Longarm's knees as a bullet intended for him buried itself in the roan's skull.

Colt already in hand he kicked, jamming his free foot against the seat of the big stock saddle and shoving with all his strength to drag his boot loose. The ambusher had been lying in wait somewhere on the slope. Longarm could hear him. His finger tightened on the trigger.

"This is Deputy Marshal Custis Long," Longarm called out in a clear, calm voice. "You can give yourself up and live to see the inside of a courtroom. Or you can take the other way out. Up to you."

TABOR EVANS

LONGARM

IN THE VALLEY OF DEATH

JOVE BOOKS, NEW YORK

LONGARM IN THE VALLEY OF DEATH

A Jove Book/published by arrangement with
the author

PRINTING HISTORY
Jove edition / July 1988

ISBN: 0-515-09647-4

Jove books are published by The Berkley Publishing Group,
200 Madison Avenue, New York, New York 10016.
The name "JOVE" and the "J" logo
are trademarks belonging to Jove Publications, Inc.

PRINTED IN THE UNITED STATES OF AMERICA

10 9 8 7 6 5 4 3 2 1

Chapter 1

Longarm leaned back in his chair, pulled out a cheroot and lit it. He stretched out, crossed his boots, and exhaled slowly.

He had finished his lunch, but he was in no hurry to return to the dull paperwork at the U.S. Marshal's office in the Federal Building two blocks away. Besides, the view was better here.

The café had opened two weeks ago, or so he was told, while he was in Wyoming Territory serving warrants. The new eatery had been opened, happily enough, by a widowed lady and her two daughters. The two girls were pretty. For that matter, their mother wasn't so bad herself. A little gray showing in her hair, true, but she was still slim and attractive. To put icing onto the top of that cake, the woman could even cook. Longarm was thinking he just might become a regular here.

"More coffee, sir?"

"Yes, thanks."

The girl gave him a smile as well as a refill, and Longarm was feeling rather full of himself when she returned to the kitchen, where her mother and sister were working to satisfy the appetites of the noontime crowd.

Longarm was not vain—far from it—but he was satisfied. Personally he could never quite understand what it was that women seemed to approve of when they looked at him. He never found anything of particular interest in the mirror when he shaved. But it was undeniable that at least some women, enough women, seemed to like what they saw when he was around.

He was tall, with a horseman's lean build. Brown hair

and a full, sweeping mustache to match. Tanned features that were more rugged than handsome. Narrow hips and wide shoulders. Clear, bright, blue-gray eyes.

His normal working attire as U.S. Marshal Billy Vail's best deputy was a tweed coat, brown corduroy trousers, black stovepipe boots, and a snuff-brown Stetson hat with a flat, telescoped crown. He usually wore a vest with a gold chain draped across his flat stomach. The chain was no affectation. Its "fob" was a .44-caliber hideout derringer, not nearly so obvious as the big .45 Colt Thunderer that virtually always rode in a cross-draw holster just to the left of his belt buckle. In Denver, though, no one looked askance at a man who chose to go armed.

Altogether ordinary in Deputy Custis Long's opinion. But he did not at all mind if an attractive lady wished to disagree with him.

He inhaled deeply from the excellent leaf of his cheroot, admired the looks of the sister who was waiting on two clerkish-looking men at the next table, and enjoyed another sip of his coffee.

"Marshal Long?"

He quit admiring the girl and turned to look instead at a man—or boy—still young enough to have pimples on a beardless face.

"Do I know you, son?"

"No, sir. Not exactly. I'm running messages for the Fed'ral Court clerk, but I'm kinda new on the job. I've seen you in the halls, though. My name's Jimmy."

Longarm nodded and smiled at the boy. He used the heel of one boot to kick a chair out from the table. "Sit down if you like, Jimmy."

"Thank you, but I'm supposed to fetch you back to the marshal's office. Quick."

"Oh?" Longarm was already reaching for his hat, the pretty waitresses and their mother forgotten. "Trouble?"

"I wouldn't know, sir. I was just told to get you."

Longarm dropped a half-dollar onto the table to more than cover the cost of his lunch and left the restaurant in a

2

loose, long-legged stride. The messenger had to hurry to keep up with him.

"How'd you know where to find me?" He had not told anyone where he was going for lunch.

"Somebody said . . . well . . . you know. Them good-lookin' girls an' everything."

"If you say so." The truth was that Longarm found it amusing. Apparently he had more of a reputation around the Federal Building than that of a manhunter.

Jimmy was already puffing. He must have run to perform his errand. The boy slowed, and Longarm left him behind. There would have to be good reason for Billy to send for him during the lunch break.

Longarm trotted briskly up the stone steps to the front doors on Colfax Avenue and hurried on to the marshal's offices. There was no sign of Vail's clerk in the outer office—Henry was probably at lunch himself—so Longarm went on into Billy's private office without knocking.

Billy Vail was there, cherubic, pink-cheeked and balding, seeming anything but the accomplished lawman he was. Longarm was not surprised to find his boss working through a lunch hour when the political hacks would be pleased to take their leisure. No one had given Billy Vail his position with the Justice Department. Billy had damn well earned it.

Vail looked up and grunted when Longarm came in. "So you were at the new café."

Longarm shrugged. "If that's what you called me back for . . ." He knew it was not.

"Sit down, dammit." Vail shuffled through the papers that littered his desk, selected a yellow Western Union message form, and shoved it across the polished surface toward Long. "This came in twenty minutes ago."

The message was brief. An officer and a sergeant assigned to the supply depot at Fort Union, New Mexico Territory, had been shot to death while conducting official business in Trinidad, state of Colorado. The commanding officer at Union was requesting Justice Department assistance in apprehending the murderer.

3

Longarm read the form through a second time and tossed it back to Vail. "Not big on detail, is he?"

"My guess is that he doesn't have much detail. It only happened last night. Do you know Colonel Howard?"

Longarm shook his head.

"I do. Good man. He would handle it himself, I imagine, if the murders had occurred on federally administered territory down in New Mexico. Since it was on this side of the line he'll avoid any political fuss by passing the problem to us. Entirely appropriate, of course. There's no question that we have jurisdiction on this one since those men were there on official business. He emphasizes that, you'll notice. Bright man, Howard."

Longarm nodded. Jurisdictional concerns always had to be taken into consideration when federal officers were operating on state lands.

"I want you to take the next train south," Billy Vail said. "The quicker you get on the scene the better."

Again Longarm nodded. Murders are often solved quickly or not at all. With the passage of time witnesses disappear and memories fade. At times money changes hands to make sure that is so. The usual run of these things, though, was for long periods of time to elapse between a crime and a request for federal assistance. Getting onto a case this quickly was practically a bonus for a U.S. deputy. The colonel at Fort Union was helpful indeed.

"I'm packed as usual," Longarm said. "All I have to do is stop at the rooming house long enough to grab my bag and head for the D.&R.G. depot."

Vail sorted through his papers and found another to push across the desk. "I have a Party or Parties Unknown warrant you can carry with you. It will do until you get a name. Wire me as soon as you know, and I'll send a proper warrant down to you."

"With any kind of luck I'll be back here tomorrow morning with your 'Party or Parties Unknown' in cuffs, and we won't have to worry about it."

Billy Vail smiled. "Want to make a small wager on that, Deputy?"

4

Longarm grinned back at his boss. "You know better. More important, *I* know better."

"Get at it then, Longarm. If I remember correctly, you have an hour and a quarter to make the next southbound."

Longarm sprang to his feet and got. An hour and a quarter was cutting it close—unless he could find a willing cab driver very quickly—and Billy Vail was *never* one to remember things incorrectly.

Chapter 2

Trinidad is a straight shot south from Denver on the Denver and Rio Grande right-of-way, a hundred fifty miles, more or less. Even at more than twenty miles per hour it was late night before the puffer came to a clattering, brake-squealing halt with the conductor moving through the cars announcing, "Trinidad, Trinidad, all out for the last stop in Colorado. Trinidad."

Sleepy passengers stirred and groaned, and some cursed the conductor for the interruption. Longarm stepped over the legs of the hemp-and-cable salesman who was snoring beside him—it had been a blessing when the talkative and lonely traveler had finally dropped off—and retrieved his hat from the overhead rack.

He made his way to the door by the dim light of a low-trimmed lamp and reminded the conductor, "I have gear in the baggage car."

"Take your time, sonny. We have to hook on two spare engines to make the climb over Raton Pass. We won't be going anywhere for a while yet."

Longarm nodded and stepped down into the cool, refreshing night. There was a smell of smoke and cinders in the air, but it was a relief to get out of the stuffy, crowded car and stretch his legs.

He smiled as he walked back to the baggage car to claim his carpetbag and saddle. It was not everyday that he was called 'sonny' anymore. And the conductor hadn't been all *that* old himself.

Longarm yawned into his fist and pointed out his things for the young fellow who was in charge of the boxes and crates and suitcases that were jumbled together in the bag-

6

gage car. The railroader handed them over quickly, and it occurred to Long that a thief could likely make a good living simply by approaching sleepy baggage handlers and claiming whatever bags struck his fancy. Fortunately it would not be a federal matter if anyone did get into such.

"Thanks." He carried his things away from the brightly lighted depot into the near-total darkness of Trinidad's streets.

Few lights showed so late at this end of town. There was a hotel in the next block with a night lamp burning inside. Longarm pushed the door open and deposited his gear by the registration desk. There was no sign of a clerk.

"Anybody home?" He tapped a bell on the counter, waited several minutes, and tried again.

"Hold your horses, dammit, I'm coming." A grumpy, balding man wearing galluses over his long johns finally put in an appearance. "What the hell do you want?"

"A room was what I had in mind," Longarm told him mildly.

"At this hour?"

"It seems a good idea."

The desk clerk grumbled and complained some more, but he dragged out the guest register, turned it to face Longarm, and dropped a key onto the counter between them. "Dollar a night," he said. "In advance. An' no loud parties."

Longarm paid. "You wouldn't be able to point the way to the town marshal's office, would you?"

"At this hour?"

"Do we have to go through this again?"

The man rubbed his eyes, gave quick, curt directions, and stumbled away to his bed in a back room.

Longarm carried his bag and saddle upstairs, left them in the plain but clean room he found with the proper number lettered on the door, and went downstairs again. The night clerk was not in evidence, but the man had been back long enough to place a Closed sign on the countertop. Longarm smiled and went outside. He hoped the local law was not so set on the idea of a full night's sleep.

7

The town marshal's office was two blocks north of the hotel. Longarm had no trouble finding it.

There was no lamp burning, but the door was open. Longarm knocked on it sharply before he went inside. He did not want to startle anyone who might come awake with a gun in his hand.

"Hello? Is anyone here?"

He pulled out a cheroot, nipped the top of it off with his teeth, and spat out the bit of tobacco. He struck a match to light his smoke and by its light found a lamp as well.

The lamplight revealed a cot at the side of the room, made up with sheet and blankets but empty at the moment.

"Damn," Longarm muttered. He had hoped to avoid delaying the start of his investigation until tomorrow.

"Something I can do for you, mister?" A burly man in a high-collared blue coat and blue cap was standing in the doorway. He wore a very small, nickel-plated revolver in a pouch strapped awkwardly high on his waist.

"I was looking for the marshal," Longarm said.

The man nodded. "You found 'im."

Longarm smiled and introduced himself.

The Trinidad marshal shoved his hand out to shake and said, "I'm Sam Tevis. All the law there is hereabouts until we get a new county sheriff appointed. And you'd be here about the soldiers that got shot last night."

The smile turned into a grin. "That's right. And I'm beginning to get the impression that you know your business, Sam Tevis." The man might not be a gunman, but he was no fool. His attitude seemed to be one of welcome rather than jealousy. That was not something a federal deputy always found when he dealt with local peace officers.

Tevis grinned back at him. "Ought to by now. I been at it one place or another since I been old enough to pick up a stick and whop a bigger fella with it. Sit down, Deputy. I know you're on duty, but I just finished my final round for the night. Care to join me for a drink?"

"That's nice of you, Sam. And I'd be pleased if you'd call me Longarm."

Tevis brought a bottle and two reasonably clean glasses

8

out of a desk drawer and poured. The bottle, Longarm noticed, was rye whiskey. This Tevis fellow had taste.

"Thanks." The rye was even of a good quality. Longarm definitely liked this man. "Smoke?"

"No. Never learned to enjoy that vice. Just as well. I like all the others good enough that I need to leave myself some running room." Tevis finished his drink, poured himself another, and topped off Longarm's glass. "Now then, Longarm, what can I tell you?"

"Everything you know. The wire we got was short on details if heavy on quick, thank goodness."

"I know what you mean. Quick is best. Not that you'll have any trouble with this one. I had half a dozen eye witnesses to the shooting, and I'm personally acquainted with the man that did the shooting, dammit."

"Dammit?"

"Yes. Dammit." Tevis sighed. "A lawman from over in the San Luis valley. Or he used to be. He's been working as a range detective lately. Hired by the Southern Colorado Cattlemen's Protective Association. Know anything about them, Longarm?"

"Some," Long admitted noncommittally. He did not want to raise any sore points with Marshal Tevis in case the man was one of those who believed—like the Association did—that a cow's life was worth more than a man's and—much more important from Longarm's viewpoint—that it was perfectly all right to conduct private executions on the strength of suspicion alone. Longarm happened to believe that the system of trial before punishment was a fair and reasonable one.

Tevis smiled, obviously guessing at the things Longarm did not say. "I know, I know. Some of these outfits have a bad name. Some of them have earned no better. But I sure never thought Tom Ferris would go that way. I figured him to be one of the better ones. Bring 'em in alive and stand 'em up to trial. Now, well, now I'm not so sure. Another?"

Longarm nodded, and Tevis poured again.

"Ferris, you say?"

"That's right. Tom Ferris. Mostly known as Major

9

Ferris. He was a major in the regular army. Not one of the quickie wartime commissions either, but an Academy man."

"It sounds like you know him pretty well."

"Well enough. We worked together a time or two when he was lawing over at Alamosa. I mean, my wants would try and run over to that side of the Peaks for him to pick up, and his would run to this side for me to pick up. We exchanged prisoners fairly often and got pretty well acquainted." He frowned. "Or I thought we did."

"So what went wrong last night?"

"That's what I can't really understand, Longarm. Tom hadn't been in town long. I'm sure of that because he hadn't come by here to say hello, and I hadn't heard anything about him being around. I never saw him myself last night, but I'm not the only one in Trinidad who knew him. He always stayed at the same place when he was here. They knew him too. An' that's where the shooting took place.

"The place is mostly a saloon, but they rent rooms too. The soldier boys had checked in there too. A shavetail lieutenant and a sergeant major with a sleeve full of enlistment stripes who was nursemaiding the young officer. They'd told the bartender there—you can talk to him yourself, of course—that they were here to do something about an army contract for coal. I don't know what, exactly, but the army buys a lot of coal that ships through Fort Union, and of course that's mostly what we live on around here is our coal mining."

Longarm nodded. None of that was news to him.

"Anyway, the two soldiers had checked into their rooms and came downstairs. Tom Ferris was in the bar, but George—that's the bartender, George Anaya—says he wasn't drinking. George says he was acting awful strange, though. Says Tom's face was . . . slack is the way George puts it. Loose. Like he was already dead drunk or sleep-walking or something. But he hadn't been drinking. George spoke to him and offered him a drink, but he says there wasn't any smell of liquor on him. Yet he acted drunk. Odd. Really odd for the Tom Ferris I know. And

10

George says he held himself stiff the way a drunk will and just stared straight ahead. Like his eyes weren't focused on anything in particular. When George offered him that drink, Tom didn't even speak to him. Just stared straight ahead like he didn't hardly know George was standing right there in front of him.

"Then George went back behind the bar to pour a beer for a customer, and that was when the soldiers came downstairs. George remembers that one of them—the sergeant, he thinks—stumbled on the bottom step and stomped his boot hard on the floor when he caught himself. Made a loud noise doing it, anyway.

"And that was when Tom Ferris hauls out his pistol and empties the thing into those two soldier boys. They hadn't done a thing to Tom. Probably never noticed him standing there and sure never provoked him any way. Yet he ups and empties his pistol into them. No warning. No reason. Nothing." Tevis frowned and finished his drink, pouring both glasses full again before he went on.

"What's even stranger, if such a thing is possible, is that after he shot them Tom didn't act like he even knew he'd done it. He turned around like nothing at all had happened, stuck his revolver back in his holster, and walked out. A man who might have been Ferris, or at least was dressed like him, was seen a little while later riding north out of town. But except for that, when Tom left the bar was the last time anyone in Trinidad saw him. He left his things in the room above George's bar. Saddlebags, a few pieces of spare clothing, box of .44-40 cartridges, and a Kennedy repeater in .45-60 caliber and cartridges to go with it, too. I have all those in the back room if you want them for anything."

Longarm shook his head. With so many witnesses and identifications of the killer, such articles were junk instead of evidence, and he did not want to be burdened with them.

"After it was over and Tom was gone," Tevis said, "somebody ran and fetched me, of course. The sergeant was killed outright, but we did what we could for the officer. He lasted a couple hours before he died. Meantime I'd got a wire off to Union telling them what happened and asking that they get help from your office."

Longarm raised an eyebrow. That was damned well unusual.

"Hell, Longarm, I'm a one-man force here. We can't even afford a night deputy for me. And like I said, we're between county sheriffs now. Bubba Crowley had a well shaft cave in on him, and the commissioners haven't appointed a replacement yet. I can't take time away from this town to go off on a long chase after Tom Ferris. And truth to tell, Longarm, if I could take the time for it, well, I'd just as soon it was somebody else who has to snap the iron onto Tom's wrists. I've liked the man long as I've known him. An' given a choice in the matter..." The Trinidad marshal spread his hands and shrugged.

"I can understand that, Sam. I don't blame you a lick, and it really is in our jurisdiction. No reason you should have to handle it."

"I appreciate you saying that, Longarm. Truly I do."

Tevis offered another refill, but this time Longarm declined. "I have to go back to the depot and get a wire off to Marshal Vail. He'll want to get the proper warrant sworn out first thing in the morning now that we have a name for the killer. You said Ferris rode north out of here?"

"If it was him, yes. I'm fairly sure it was, actually. My guess would be that he's headed back to LaVeta Pass to cross over to the San Luis."

"And he was town marshal at Fort Garland, right?"

"Until eight, nine months ago. That's when he went over to the SCCPA. I don't know why, exactly. The new man at Garland isn't so friendly as Tom always was, and what little business we've had has been conducted mostly at arm's length."

Longarm smiled and extended his hand. "Sam Tevis, it's been a real pleasure meeting you, and I'll be happy if we can work together sometime. Believe me, if all state and local peace officers were as good as you, my job would be a hell of a lot easier."

12

Tevis seemed genuinely pleased by the compliment. But then Longarm had meant every word of it.

Longarm went back outside and headed down the dark street toward the railroad station. He wanted that wire to be waiting on Billy's desk when the marshal got in in the morning.

Chapter 3

Longarm dumped his gear on the depot platform and found the telegrapher's office at the Walsenburg station north of Trinidad.

"No, sir," the telegrapher told him. "No messages here for you and no envelope."

"Damn," Longarm muttered. Billy's early-morning wire, catching him before he left Trinidad, said the warrant for Major Thomas Ferris's arrest would be coming on the first available train and should catch him in Walsenburg, where Long would have to switch from rail to coach for the climb over LaVeta Pass and back down into the San Luis Valley at Fort Garland.

A schedule posted outside said the next southbound would not be coming through for several hours.

"You don't know when the next coach west is leaving, do you?" Longarm asked.

"As a matter of fact I do, sir," the operator said. "There's only one coach a day goes that way. Leaves every morning at ten sharp." He smiled. "Or close to sharp, anyhow."

A clock on the wall over the telegraph key showed it was already 9:23. According to that, Longarm had less than forty minutes to make his connection or wait until tomorrow. And railroad station clocks were generally accurate, dammit.

Longarm thanked the telegrapher and went to find the D.&R.G.'s local manager. He explained his problem, and the railroader assured him, "I'll forward your package on tomorrow's stage, Marshal. Be no problem at all."

"Thanks." Longarm retrieved his saddle and bag and

14

headed across the street to the South Plains and San Luis Express Company office. He still had time to catch the westbound stage and avoid falling another complete day behind the killer. And he still had the Party or Parties Unknown warrant in his coat pocket. It would do for the time being.

The stage company clerk honored his travel pass and issued him a ticket without complaint. Some of the small lines, those that lacked government mail contracts, demanded payment even from federal officers, a few of them going so far as to refuse government vouchers and requiring cash.

The coach itself was a light mud wagon with benches installed to accommodate up to ten passengers. Flimsy side curtains without isinglass were rolled and tied at intervals around the open bodywork of the wagon in case they ran into foul weather. There was no shotgun guard on a peaceful run like this one, and the four-up team were all light and leggy animals.

"Will that bunch make the pull?" Longarm asked as he handed the driver his ticket and deposited his things in the luggage boot slung on the rear of the wagon.

"Hell, no." The driver spat a stream of brown juice onto the spokes of the rear wheel. "We'll make a change before we start up. Comp'ny keeps a string of big boys over there for the serious hauling."

Longarm nodded and crawled into the empty coach, choosing a forward-facing seat at the back. The front bench faced the rear, and in the middle was a pair of short benches placed back-to-back. For the time being he was the only passenger aboard. He was joined a few minutes later by two well-dressed men who apparently knew each other, and by a taciturn, sloppily dressed cowboy who looked like he was on the tail end of an extended drunk. The cowboy sprawled across the front bench, closed his eyes, and almost immediately began to snore. The businessmen took the other forward facing seats in the middle, leaving Longarm alone at the back of the rig.

The driver disappeared inside the depot and came back

out a moment later with a mail pouch. He deposited the mail on the floor of the driving box and climbed onto the high seat.

"Anybody with a change o' mind better speak up now." He released the brake, then picked up his whip and popped it in the air between the leaders. The coach rocked into motion.

"Thanks. Don't mind if I do." Longarm pushed his cup forward, and the businessman tipped his flask over it. Longarm and the two businessmen were inside the relay station having a quick lunch of bacon sandwiches and strong coffee. The driver was outside supervising the team change. The cowboy was presumably still snoring the day away in the coach. They had shaken him awake when they stopped, but the mention of food had turned him visibly pale and he had not wanted to come inside with the others.

"My pleasure," the businessman said and tilted the flask over his friend's cup and his own.

"Are you gentlemen local?" Longarm asked.

"From the San Louie, if that's what you mean," one of them agreed. "We deal in hardware and farm-an'-ranch supplies. I'm from Alamosa, myself. Howard here is from Fort Garland. We're on our way home from a sales presentation in Pueblo. New kind of bob wire. The manufacturer is all hot to prove how his wire is better than anybody else's."

"He ought to be," Howard said. "He's the one stands to make the profit if we sell it for him."

"Interesting," Longarm fibbed. "You say you're from Fort Garland?"

"That's right."

"You wouldn't know a man there by the name of Ferris, would you? Tom Ferris?"

"The major? Of course I know the man. Not as a customer, you understand, but he was our town marshal for, oh, a year, year and a half. Something like that. Of course I know him."

"They tell me he isn't lawing there anymore." Longarm

16

took a sip of the stoutly laced coffee and decided it wasn't bad, whatever the other hardware dealer had put into it.

"That's right. He, uh, got a better offer, I expect."

Longarm smiled at Howard. "Something in the way you say that makes me think there might be more to it than just a better offer."

Howard shrugged and looked like he intended to say no more on the subject.

"I'm not meaning to pry," Longarm assured him. "I have a reason to ask." He pulled out his wallet and showed his badge.

"The major went and got himself in trouble, did he?" Howard sounded like he hoped that was the case.

"That isn't for me to decide," Longarm said. "I need to look him up and get some information from him."

Howard glanced around to make sure they were not overheard, though he was obviously not concerned about his friend from Alamosa listening in. "I think you'll find, Marshal, that Ferris has a lot of friends around Garland still. Except for men with daughters to be thinking about, that is."

"Oh?"

"Uh-huh. Nice man, I expect, in a lot of ways, but he's the horniest son of a bitch I ever seen. I caught him making eyes one time at my eldest. Hell, the child's only eighteen. Didn't make any difference to him, though. He was sniffing around her like a dog in heat. But I set him straight about that, let me tell you. Told him I'd take a ten gauge and blow his pecker to red mush with it if he didn't leave be. He never come around her after that, he didn't."

"I don't blame you," Longarm said, although to himself he had to wonder if it had ever occurred to this Howard that it takes two to strike that particular bargain. "You were saying something about Ferris losing his job at Garland?" Which of course was not exactly what Howard had been saying, but . . .

"Damn right he did. He was a pretty good lawman for a spell. I got to say that much about him. He did all right with his badge for a while. But then he got to drinking on the sly. At least that's what I figure it was. Acted drunk sometimes, though I can't say that anybody ever actually saw him drink all that much. But he began to act like he was drunk. Or crazy, maybe. Not so much at first, but then it got worse and worse, till finally you couldn't depend on the man at all. The topper was one time a bunch of cowboys rode in from the Six Bar outfit and got likkered up and terrorizing the girls at the Red Hat. That wouldn't have been so bad, I suppose, but there were some decent gentlemen in the place at the time, and these boys were causing an uproar. What they needed was to be put in the cells till they sobered up and got to their senses again. But when one of our town councilmen went to get Ferris, Ferris didn't want to be bothered with it. Can you imagine that? Didn't want to be bothered. And when the councilman insisted, Ferris shoved him, shoved him right down and then walked off like nothing had happened at all. Can you imagine that?"

"No," Longarm said sympathetically, "I certainly can't."

Howard frowned. "That was the end of him, of course. We couldn't have any more of that go on. Actually pushing a council member. He'd been all right for a long time, though, so they let him resign instead of firing him outright."

"How long ago was this?"

"Oh, I don't remember for sure. This past winter, it was. Call it five months or thereabouts."

The man from Alamosa emptied his flask over the three cups, and the two hardware dealers went back to talking about barbed wire and whether this new product was really an improvement over what they were already selling.

It was a subject that was not high on Longarm's list of interests, so he arranged a polite expression on his tanned face and thought over what Howard had said while the other men talked.

It fit, of course, with what Sam Tevis had told him back in Trinidad.

And really it was something that a prosecutor would

have to worry about much more than a deputy marshal should. Longarm's job was to find Thomas Ferris and place him under arrest. A court of law would have to sort out the why of it all if they chose to do so.

The driver stuck his head inside to call out that the coach was ready for the pull up LaVeta Pass. Longarm and the businessmen finished their drinks and went out into the harsh sunshine. It was a fine day, and handsome country with the twin knobs of the Spanish Peaks looming to the south.

With luck, Longarm thought, he would have Ferris in cuffs before dark and be on his way back to Denver when the next coach pulled east from Fort Garland.

Chapter 4

This end of the San Luis Valley was ranching country. Farther west where there was more water available the land was largely used for farming. And beyond that in the huge bowl that lay between the Sangre de Cristos and San Juans, the foothills and marginal lands were given heavily to sheep and even some goat herds.

Despite its name there was no fort at Fort Garland, nor had there been any troops there for years, at least to the best of Longarm's knowledge. Soldiers had been posted there during the Mexican War and again, briefly, during the last serious Ute outbreak.

It was dusk when the stagecoach rocked to a halt in the middle of the small town.

"Half-hour stop," the driver called. Another team of light horses was led out to take the place of the heavy cobs they had been using since the stop on the other side of LaVeta.

The man named Howard shook hands with his friend who was traveling on, nodded to Longarm, and hurried off toward a waiting carriage with a middle-aged woman and collection of teenaged children in it.

Longarm stretched, beat some of the dust off his trouser legs, and watched while the cowboy who had accompanied them from Walsenburg—awake and sober now—ankled in the direction of the nearest saloon. Apparently it wouldn't do for the fellow to remain sober too long.

The tall deputy had a pleasantly virtuous feeling when he claimed his luggage and carried it toward the town marshal's office he could see in the next block.

"Marshal Grenville," the local lawman said after Longarm introduced himself. Grenville did not rise or offer to shake hands. He was propped in a chair with his boot heels on his desk and a plate of soupy goulash in his lap. The front of his shirt showed that he had already started his supper before Longarm interrupted.

"I need to see the former marshal here," Longarm said. "A Major Thomas Ferris."

"I'm the law here now," Grenville said.

"Yes, but it's Ferris I need to see." On the long drive from Walsenburg Longarm had decided it might not be wise to say too much about the business he had with the former town marshal. Among the many things Howard had said was that Ferris still had friends here.

Grenville frowned. "You won't find him here."

"By 'here' do you mean I won't find him in Fort Garland, or that I won't find him in this office?" Longarm tried a smile to see if that would help soften the scowling local. It didn't.

"Means I cain't help you. Now was there somethin' else you have to bother me with or can I go back to my dinner?"

"Thank you for your cooperation, *Marshal* Grenville." He turned and got the hell out of there before Grenville said something more. Longarm was riding the thin edge of anger for some reason, and there was no point to that.

No wonder Sam Tevis dealt with Grenville only at arm's length. The two men were both local peace officers, but they were about as different as horses and horse turds. And Longarm had a definite opinion as to which was which in that particular comparison.

There would be no eastbound stage until tomorrow morning, no matter what else happened here at Garland—they had passed the stage company's eastbound shortly after starting up the pass this afternoon—so Longarm carried his things to the single hotel he saw on Fort Garland's main street and checked into a room for the night.

"There's a chance I might be meeting a friend here," Longarm said. "I assume you can put a cot in if need be."

"For twenty cents extra, I can," the clerk told him.

"I'll let you know. Thanks."

He deposited his saddle and bag in the room and went back outside to find some supper before he got serious about looking for Major Ferris. If the man had come here after he left Trinidad he would still be here later. If not, there was no need to hurry anyway.

The nearest café was in the same business block as the stage stop at the edge of town. It was getting a fair patronage from the locals, so it probably would be as good a choice as any.

The place was run by a pudgy, red-faced, middle-aged woman and a fat, slatternly-looking younger woman. Longarm saw no comparison whatsoever with the new café near the Federal Building in Denver. Both these 'ladies' looked greasy enough that a man might slide right off if he ever got desperate enough to want to jump one of them.

"Regular supper?" the younger one asked after he was seated.

"That kinda depends on what a regular supper happens to be."

"Steak. Fried taters. Applesauce. Rolls hot outa the oven. All the butter you want to heap on anything. Coffee."

"A regular supper," Longarm agreed.

When the meal came he decided that these old gals weren't so bad after all. Hell, there is more than one way a woman can please a man. And these two had the cooking side of it whipped.

When he was done with the rest of it the girl brought him a slab of warm, dried apple pie served in a bowl and with a pitcher of cream alongside. Longarm was tempted to fall in love.

"You don't look so busy right now," he said before she could get away. "Maybe you could help me."

"Yes, sir?"

"I'm looking for Major Tom Ferris. I understand he isn't the marshal here anymore, but I was hoping he would still be in town."

The fat girl smiled and there was a softness in her eyes

22

when Ferris's name was mentioned. "Sure wish I *could* help you, mister, but I ain't seen Tom—the major, I mean —in a couple weeks."

"Thanks."

Whatever memory it was that put the dreamy look into the unattractive girl's eyes was still there when she went back toward the kitchen.

Longarm watched her go and managed somehow to keep from shaking his head at the sight of her. Damn. Maybe that Howard fella hadn't been exaggerating after all when he said Tom Ferris was a horny so-and-so. He would have to be to put that kind of look onto the face of a girl that homely.

Longarm paid for his supper, lit a cheroot, and strolled out onto the street.

It was fully dark by now, but still early enough in the evening that the saloons and even a few stores were still doing business.

If Ferris was in town someone had to have seen him arrive. A saloon was the most likely place to learn if it was true. Longarm decided to start at one end of Garland and work his way to the other.

Chapter 5

If Major Tom Ferris was back in town, no one seemed to have seen him. Longarm got a nope from the bartender of the second saloon he had looked into, and turned to leave without the courtesy of buying a beer to pay for the man's helpfulness. Before long the word would get around that there was a man in Garland looking for the ex-marshal. Longarm did not want Ferris spooked in case that word found the man before Longarm did.

He stopped at the door of the saloon and stepped out of the way as the cowboy who had been on the stage from Walsenburg pushed past him in a big hurry to get to the fresh air.

The cowboy had sobered during the course of the drive, but that problem had been corrected by now. The man must have been drinking steadily while Longarm was tending to his business here, because by now he was as thoroughly soused as he had been when he crawled blindly into the coach back on the plains.

Longarm watched without sympathy while the cowboy tried to heave into the dirt of the street, bringing up nothing but a few strings of mucus and spittle for his efforts.

Long couldn't help wondering if the fellow was having fun.

The cowboy staggered off up the street in the same direction Longarm was going. Longarm stayed where he was long enough to get a cheroot lit and drawing well rather than follow too closely behind the sloppy drunk.

A storefront was lighted in the next block, apparently still open for business. Longarm headed toward it. If Ferris was not showing himself in the saloons he still might be in

24

town. The storekeeper might have seen him.

The cowboy walking ahead of Longarm stumbled on the step from the street onto the plank sidewalk, made a wild grab at the post supporting a half-roof over the walk, and somehow managed to keep going without falling down. Longarm shook his head and trailed idly along behind the man.

A young woman appeared at the door to the store, turned to say something to someone inside, and started out onto the walk just as the drunk reached the spot too.

They collided, the drunk walking blindly into her without slowing.

The girl yelped and would have fallen except the cowboy was hanging on to her trying to support himself. Between them they remained upright but unstable.

"Are you all right?" The girl was laughing and did not seem offended by the unintended clumsiness of the drunk. "You can let go now." She paused. "Please let go now."

Longarm increased his stride.

"Please let go of me now." This time there was a note of concern in her voice.

The cowboy blinked owlishly, grinned, and drooled spittle down his chin. One hand was resting perilously close to the girl's breast. He grinned again, shifted his hand and squeezed. "Honk. Honk honk." He began to cackle.

The girl paled and went stiff.

Longarm came up behind the drunk, took him by the back of the neck, and hauled him off the girl.

"Beshie? Beshie?"

Longarm was not sure but thought the cowboy might have been trying to say Bessie.

"Huh-uh, fella. Wrong lady. Go sleep this off, why don't you." He turned the drunk around, stepped him down off the sidewalk, and gave him a push in the direction of an alley across the street.

The cowboy staggered across the street, climbed onto the opposite sidewalk, and curled himself into a ball on a public bench outside the bank building.

Longarm made sure the fellow was not going to cause

any more trouble, then turned back to the girl and touched his hat brim. "Sorry, ma'am. I wish I'd been a little quicker."

"No harm done," she said. She glanced back inside the store to where a man behind the counter was watching, a hickory ax handle in his hands but not needed now. "Thank you, Mr. Petrick." Petrick nodded and returned the ax handle to a barrel of them offered for sale.

"And thank you, sir," she said.

She was giving Long a thorough looking over by the light from the store windows. Longarm got the impression that she liked what she was seeing.

"My pleasure, miss." The girl looked vaguely familiar for some reason. He could not imagine why.

"Would you be kind enough to walk with me? I . . . wouldn't want to be accosted again."

"Of course, miss."

She smiled and started down the sidewalk slowly. "My, polite as well as handsome."

"Ma'am?"

She looked back to see that they were well away from the storefront where Petrick or a customer might have overheard. "You *are* my fair knight are you not, sir?"

"Well . . ."

She laughed. "Don't be shy now. You rescued me. Now aren't you obligated to carry me off to live happily ever after?"

Longarm had no idea how in hell he was supposed to respond to something like that. The girl was pretty enough, but was she a little off in the head?

She laughed again and tucked her arm inside the crook of his elbow, leaning against him so that her hip was in contact with his thigh. "I'm not being *serious,* you know. Just playful. I hope you don't mind."

"Not at all."

"Good." She snuggled closer to him. "You are terribly handsome, you know. And I've been *terribly* bored lately."

"Look. Miss. I don't know exactly what—"

"Simple," she interrupted. "You are tall and handsome.

I am passionate and bored. Best of all you're a stranger in town, so you won't do something dreary like wanting to slobber all over me forever and ever afterward. I was thinking we might go up to your hotel room and do a bit of friendly fucking with no strings attached." She gave him a smile of sweet innocence.

Custis Long hadn't been shocked by anything in years. Exactly. But he came damned close to it when the girl's words sank in.

"Well?" she asked.

"How is it you know I have a hotel room here?"

"I saw you come outside a little while ago. Would you like me to tell you where you had supper?"

"I . . . don't think that would be necessary."

"All right. So. Do you want a roll in the hay or not? I warn you, I take at least as much as I give. But I give an *awful* lot, honey."

"It wouldn't be very polite of me to turn you down, now would it?"

"I did say you were polite as well as handsome, didn't I?"

"I believe you did at that."

"But not very gallant. Surely you can think of a better reason than politeness." She half turned, rubbing her breasts against his arm and laughing lightly.

"Mm, I just might be able to find some reasons at that."

"Good. What's your room number?"

He told her.

"I'll meet you there in, oh, an hour." She giggled. "There is a back door they never lock. The one going to the backhouse. Leave your room door unlocked too, and I'll slip in with no one the wiser but you and me." She gave his arm a tight squeeze and turned to run lightly across the street and into the shadows.

Damn, Longarm thought.

Unbelievable.

But he could still feel the firm, warm thrust of her breasts brushing against his arm and the solid feel of her hip against him.

27

He had to wonder if she really intended to come or if this was some sort of game she played with strange men in town.

Still, there was no doubt that she acted like she knew exactly what she was doing, exactly how she could sneak into the hotel without being seen.

It would have been impolite to say so out loud, but she certainly acted like this was something she had done a good many times before now.

He decided to make no assumptions about whether she would come or not. She would or she would not, and there was certainly nothing he could do about it either way.

Even so, he intended to hurry and get his questions asked at the few places that remained open in town.

Quickly enough, that is, to get him back in his room in, say, another hour.

Chapter 6

He left the room door unlocked. But he kept his Colt handy too. It was unlikely that anyone in Fort Garland had the kind of mad on with him or possibly with any federal officer that would lead to something like this as an ambush ploy. Unlikely, but not impossible. Longarm was not willing to bet his life on the length of the odds.

He sat in a corner in the one chair the hotel provided and kept the wick on the bedside lamp turned low so that he was in shadow. Just in case. His hands lay folded across his stomach, inches away from the butt of the big Colt. Just in case.

Footsteps sounded in the narrow, rugless hallway, and Longarm tensed. The footsteps were those of a man—someone much heavier than the pretty girl he had seen outside the general store—who was trying to walk lightly on his feet.

The footsteps continued past his door, however, to the next room, and he could hear a drink-slurred voice curse as the neighbor tried with scant success to insert his key into the lock. Finally there was the sound of a door opening and closing again, and he could hear the man stumbling about in a dark room on his way to bed.

Moments later he heard a slight creaking of floorboards from the direction of the hall but no sound of footsteps whatsoever. Longarm's door opened silently, and the girl ghosted inside.

She looked at him and smiled.

She was wearing a mantilla now, draped over blonde hair. She let the lacy shawl slip to her shoulders, and Longarm saw that she had unpinned her hair since he saw her on

29

the street. It fell loose and gleaming to the small of her back when she turned, deliberately posing for his inspection and obviously wanting his approval.

"Nice."

It was no lie. He noticed too that in the time since she left him earlier she had removed her confining undergarments. Her body was lush beneath a thin layer of cloth.

She gave him a coy, catlike smile and arched her back, teasing him.

Then she turned and slid the bolt closed to lock the world away.

So much for suspicions. Longarm stood.

"Is that bourbon?" She was looking at the bottle of Maryland rye he had set on the dresser.

"Rye."

"I've never had rye before."

In the dim light of the hotel room she looked younger than she had on the street. "Are you sure you're old enough to drink?"

She laughed softly. "That and more." Without waiting for an invitation she went to the dresser, pulled the cork, and helped herself to a drink straight from the bottle. She made a face. "Bourbon's better." But she drank again.

She came to him, standing close before him with her eyes bright and her moist lips slightly parted. She was breathing heavily. "Don't you want to kiss me?"

"That and more," he parroted with a straight face.

She brought her mouth up to his, her arms winding behind his neck. She tasted of rye whiskey and peppermint.

Longarm kissed her, enjoying the feel of her body against his.

She closed her eyes and captured his tongue between her lips, applying a quick, fierce suction as she drew his tongue into her mouth. After no more than seconds she began to shudder, her belly pressing against his pelvis and her breath ragged.

"Surely you didn't . . ."

"Oh, but I did." Her voice was a whisper now, husky and thick with desire.

"Damn."

"Yeah-h-h-h." She sighed and let go of him with one hand so she could fumble first at her own buttons and then at his. Not frantic now but certainly eager. "Help me?"

He lifted her and carried her to the bed, depositing her there and kneeling beside her to finish the job she had started on her buttons.

As he had suspected, she had shed her underclothing. She was naked except for the dress and her shoes, and they were quickly disposed of.

Her breasts were large, but she still had the taut firmness of youth. Her nipples were large and dark. Her pubic hair a pale, thin patch of curls.

Longarm kissed her again and ran his hands over her body. She shuddered and lifted herself to him when he probed that curly vee with a searching fingertip, finding heat and moisture there.

"Oh. Mister."

Longarm damn near ruined the whole thing by laughing. He had no idea what this girl's name was, nor obviously did she know his.

This did not seem like a time to ask personal questions.

He kissed her again and ran the tip of his tongue across her cheek, over both her eyes and down into her ear. She fumbled at his buttons again.

Longarm backed away only far enough and long enough to shed his clothes, then lay beside her on the hard, narrow bed so the heat of her flesh was pressed against him head to toe. She twined her legs into his and damn near sucked his tongue out by the roots.

He pushed his hand between her thighs, and she opened herself to him.

"More. Deeper. Please."

He pressed inside her and used the ball of his thumb to roll the tiny button of her pleasure. The girl bit his shoulder in an attempt to stifle a squeal of release that was torn out of her.

"Now," she demanded.

"So soon?"

"Now."

He obliged, rising over her while she spread her legs wide to receive him, then plunging down and in.

She moaned and began to writhe beneath him, pumping her hips frantically, spearing herself on his shaft, wrapping her arms and legs around him and drawing him even deeper while she raked his back with nails that were mercifully bitten short.

She clung to him, shoving her tongue into his ear and panting with the effort of her exertions until she exploded into the momentary relief of a climax.

When she let go she collapsed, spent and exhausted.

After a bit she opened her eyes. "You didn't, did you?"

Longarm smiled at her. "There's time. Some things are too good to hurry."

"Oh, mister, you're the best."

"Thank you, I'm sure."

"Look, uh, no offense or anything. But can you get it up more than once?"

"I think I can manage it." How the hell old did she think he was, anyway?

She grinned. "Can I taste the first time?"

"If that's what you'd like."

The grin became smug, and she wriggled out from under him. She pushed him down onto his back and knelt between his legs.

When she bent over him her hair fell in a cascade of soft gold to engulf his balls. It tickled and tantalized the insides of his thighs, and she shook her head slightly to increase the effect she was having on him.

She was a tease, by damn, but he didn't mind. Her kind of tease delivered on the promises.

She bent lower, still grinning, and gently held his cock aside so she could run her tongue over his balls. Then, holding them in the palm of her hand, she lifted her face and slowly, carefully, licked his shaft from base to head.

Longarm knew damn good and well what she wanted. She wanted to arouse him beyond control. Wanted him to demand more and more of her.

32

Instead he held himself under rigid control, forcing himself to lie immobile while she tried to wring a response from him.

She stopped for a moment, looked up at him, and winked. Longarm laughed. He could not help it.

The girl grinned in response, winked in acknowledgment that he had won, and with a sigh took him into her mouth, surrounding him with the moist heat that seemed to cut into him all the way down to his cods.

"You got about ten seconds to stop that, or . . ."

She shook her head violently from side to side, adding to the sensations she was producing down there and sending cool, soft waves of hair over his belly.

By then it was much too late. Longarm groaned and raised himself to her.

The girl stayed with him, sucking eagerly for even more. She sat up a moment later and smiled. "I sure hope you weren't teasing me about a next time. That got me to wanting it all over again."

"Come here," he said, "I'll show you."

With a giggle of delight the girl flung herself forward and sprawled onto his chest.

Longarm proved his point with considerable pleasure.

Chapter 7

Longarm yawned. This girl was certainly enjoyable, but he wanted to get some sleep too.

She sighed and cuddled closer against him. The flesh that had been so cool and soft just a little while earlier was warm and damp now, slightly sticky with a thin film of fresh sweat. Longarm stroked her back and she arched her body against his.

"Nice," she murmured.

"Mmm." He yawned again, not bothering to hide it from her. "Mind if I ask you something?"

She shook her head.

"What's your name?"

She giggled. "Lisa. Lisa Howard."

"Howard?" It came to him finally why it was she had looked familiar to him earlier. She had been in the carriage that met the stagecoach. "Your father owns the hardware store here?"

Lisa pulled a few inches away from him with a look of alarm.

"It's all right," he assured her quickly. "I won't say anything. You're eighteen and old enough to decide some things for yourself."

She settled back against his chest but not so close this time. She was beginning to become restive. Now that he knew who she was, though, Longarm was no longer in such a hurry for her to leave.

"You know Tom Ferris, don't you?" he asked.

"Lordy, mister, do you know *every*thing about me?"

"Of course not. The truth is, I heard your father complaining about Ferris chasing after you." He gave her a kiss. "Not that I blame him, you understand. You're a lot of woman, Lisa Howard." The compliment pleased her and she nuzzled his chest enough to make him think that perhaps he would not want her to leave for a little while, even after he was done talking with her.

"That's all right then," she said. "Sure, I know Tommy. He's . . . special. To tell you the truth, mister, if he was in town right now I wouldn't have been wanting to meet you." She giggled. "Like this." This time instead of kissing his chest she ran the tip of her tongue lightly over and around his nipple, sending a tingle of fresh interest deep into his groin at the delicate touch.

"Tell me about him," Longarm prompted.

She turned her head to look at him. "Why would you want to know?"

"He used to be a lawman here. I'm a lawman from Denver. I need to ask him about some things."

"Oh." The incomplete answer seemed to satisfy her. And it occurred to him that she still did not bother to ask his name. A passionate girl Lisa Howard undoubtedly was, but a curious one she was not. "What do you want to know?"

"Oh, what kind of man he is. What he looks like. The things and the places he enjoys. Most of all, where I might find him since he doesn't seem to be here right now."

Lisa's forehead wrinkled in thought. Longarm uncharitably had the impression that thought was not her long suit. While she was thinking her hand strayed idly south, cupping and lightly toying with his limp, sticky cock. It remained sticky but soon was no longer so limp as he began to get an erection again under her casual touch.

"I guess," she said finally, "the thing Tommy likes best is to fuck." She giggled. "Kinda like I do."

Longarm kissed her forehead and let her continue in her own way if she would.

"He's positively dreamy, really. It's a funny thing about that, really. I mean, he isn't actually *handsome*. Exactly. But there is something *about* him. I don't know what it is,

35

really. Kind of melancholy and romantic and dark. But exciting."

Not exactly the sort of description Billy Vail would want to put on a Wanted poster. *Wanted: Ferris, Thomas, former major U.S. Army, melancholy and darkly romantic*. No, Longarm thought, that wouldn't do. Still, he was interested in the girl's description. It could turn out to be the sort of thing that would give him a better handle on Major Ferris than any normal age, height, weight categorization.

"He's almost as tall as you," Lisa went on, "but thinner. Now that I think of it, he's really awfully skinny. Skin and bone and these huge, deep-set, pale eyes. Dark, curly hair. But none on his chest. His chest is as bare as mine." She giggled. "But flatter, of course."

Longarm responded to the implied request by stroking Lisa's chest. Hers definitely was not flat. She stretched, and for a moment her eyes went slightly out of focus at his touch. She damn sure was an easy one to arouse.

"I don't know what it is about Tommy, but he's so *intense*. I mean, when I'm with him it's like the most important thing in the world to him is me and my body. Like there isn't anything else in the whole wide world that he'd rather do than put it in me. And please me too. Maybe that's what is so special about him. He doesn't want to just poke it in me and go away. He wants to please me too. Like you do too, kinda. And believe me, mister, I appreciate that in a man. But Tommy—I don't mean any offense to you, mind—he makes love better than anybody." She giggled again. Longarm was not big on gigglers. But he was willing to make an exception now and then. "Like it was his last meal or something."

"Is, uh, Tommy your steady?"

"Oh, gosh no. I wish he was. But of course Daddy would have a fit. I mean, I can't always get away. Just sometimes. Like tonight, what with Daddy having been away at that sales thing in Pueblo, all he wanted to do tonight was take Mama upstairs." Again that giggle. It was becoming annoying. "She'll be all sore and walking spraddle-legged tomorrow. Mama doesn't like loving the way I

36

do. Lord knows, I don't know where I get it from. Must be Daddy 'cause it sure wasn't from her. She's told me so herself, how the things a husband and wife do together at night—that's the way she puts it, like she can't bear to say the word 'sex'—are a duty that the wife has to put up with. Huh. If I ever do marry, the son of a bitch *better* put it up. And plenty."

Longarm had only sympathy for whatever poor fool ended up marrying this one. As a short-term companion, though, he had few complaints.

"Most nights, though," Lisa rambled on, "Daddy wants all us kids there in the parlor with him and Mama. He likes to hear us play the piano and read poetry and stuff like that." She made a face. "Bor-r-ring."

"I can see how it would be," Longarm said.

"Stupid, really. But I like to get out whenever I can to be with Tommy. I mean, the man just doesn't *quit*. He's the horniest guy I've ever met. Can't get enough, which suits me just fine. And I know whenever I can't get away he'll take anything female that'll hold still for him. Which is most of the women and half the girls in Fort Garland, dammit."

"I suppose the best place to look for him would be in a whorehouse, then."

"Tommy? Not him. He wouldn't have to pay for it with some slut like those women." Longarm had thoughts about kettles calling pots black, but he kept the notion to himself. "Tommy's the kind of man a girl just looks at and gets all excited." She giggled again and kissed his nipples. "You have that too, whatever it is."

Longarm was all of a sudden having difficulty remembering that there was a point to this conversation.

"He's a lunger, you know," Lisa interjected from somewhere out of the blue, dragging an unwilling Longarm back to earth again.

"A consumptive?"

"That's right. A lunger. That's why he had to leave the army and move out here. For his health. A lot of people do that, you know. 'Cause it's dry here or something."

Longarm did know. Consumption was something the doctors knew little about except that it involved the lungs. And frequently a slow death. A high, dry climate often arrested the disease, but rarely if ever cured it. "Did coming here make him better?" he asked.

Lisa shrugged. "He thinks so. Sort of, anyhow. Sometimes it's better and sometimes worse. He has some medicine he takes for it, but I don't like it when he's taking his damn medicine. The stuff makes him all funny. Like he's someplace else, almost."

"Really?" Lisa was playing with him again, but this time Longarm was too interested in what she had just said to respond properly.

So this Ferris was a consumptive and was taking medicine for it. Longarm knew little enough about the subject, but he knew enough to realize that there was no medication specific to consumption. But a good many lungers used the readily available opiates as a relief measure during the sporadic outbreaks the lingering disease was prone to.

And a heavy dose of laudanum or tincture of opium or some similar drug would certainly be consistent with what he had been told about Tom Ferris's actions in Trinidad when the two Fort Union personnel were murdered.

A healthy slug of laudanum can turn a whirling dervish into a sleepwalker within minutes.

"You don't happen to know what this medicine is, do you, Lisa?"

"Naw. Something in a little brown bottle. That's all I know about it. And that I don't like it."

Longarm grunted. There almost certainly was a druggist in Fort Garland. If nothing else, one of the general merchants would sell drugs and patent medicines. It was something he could inquire about come morning.

"Look," she said, "do we have to spend all night talking about Tommy? I mean, thinking about him—and you too, mister—has got me all worked up again."

"Then why don't we do something about that, Lisa," he offered.

She giggled—dammit—and opened herself to his touch.

After that, though, she was intent on something better than giggling, and Longarm had no more time for idle nit-picking about minor personality quirks.

Chapter 8

"I am not a pharmacist," the storekeeper explained. "What you laymen would call a druggist, that is."

Pedantic old fart, Longarm thought, but he kept the amusement he was feeling from reaching his face. He knew perfectly good and well what a pharmacist was. But, hell, Mr. Petrick would not know that. Probably most of his customers would not recognize the term. Longarm kept his expression blank and his mouth shut.

"I do, however, dispense medications bottled prior to distribution. We have neither a pharmacist nor a physician —a doctor, that is—in Fort Garland. For either of those one must travel to Alamosa in the valley or out as far as Pueblo and Canon City beyond the San Luis. Or of course south to—"

"But you do sell medicines," Longarm interrupted. He was sure Petrick would be pleased to give a lesson in geography as well as one in proper English, but there were limits to how much Longarm was willing to endure in answer to a simple question.

"That is correct," Petrick said. "Was there something in particular I could help you with?"

"Yes, sir, there is. I need to know what medicines you've been selling to Major Tom Ferris."

Petrick puffed up like a pouter pigeon and gave Longarm a dirty look. "Really, sir. I do *not* discuss the confidential affairs of my clientele with perfect stran—"

Longarm had his wallet ready in anticipation of the need as soon as Petrick got that huffy look about him. He flipped it open now and laid it on the counter between them.

"Oh." Petrick clamped his jaw shut and bent forward to examine Longarm's credentials. He removed his spectacles, brought out a handkerchief, and began to polish the already-clean lenses. "I really don't know that I can. . . ."

"You can," Longarm said. He smiled.

"Is this germane to . . ."

"It is," Longarm assured him.

"But . . ."

"Please." Again he smiled. He was fairly sure if he tried to play a hard line with Petrick the stuffy storekeeper would sull up and turn stubborn on him. It really should not be necessary to threaten things like obstruction of justice charges. Particularly in a town where the asshole marshal might make it difficult for a federal officer to make good on threats to the voting locals.

"The information may be important," Longarm said. "I can promise you, though, that I will keep it entirely confidential unless it is absolutely necessary"—he smiled—"and germane to do otherwise."

Petrick harrumphed and hesitated, but he seemed to be wavering.

"I would be pleased to explain the need to you, Mr. Petrick, except that as I am sure you understand, I would not want to prejudice the good name of anyone." He made a show of looking around to see that they were not overheard, although at this early hour there were no customers in the store. "I can tell you—but please keep this to yourself, Mr. Petrick—that I suspect someone may have stolen a supply of opiates from Major Ferris and used the drugs for . . . shall we say? . . . improper purposes. And I know neither you nor I would want the major to suffer for the actions of another. Would we?"

The lie was thin and Longarm knew it. What he was hoping, and expecting really, was that Petrick would be so pleased to be in on the make-believe confidence that he would not examine the story closely. Longarm would not have said the same thing to a dull, slow-witted man who would be inclined to see things on the surface. But a man like Petrick who is convinced of his own erudition is often more easily gulled than those slower, dimmer folks he feels superior to.

Petrick harrumphed again, but this time he smiled. He too glanced around the empty store before he leaned closer to Longarm and whispered, "You will keep this strictly between us? I wouldn't want it noised about that I was telling tales about my clientele."

"Strictly between ourselves," Longarm pledged, "if it is at all possible to do so."

"Yes, well, I have been selling a regular supply of opiates to Marshal—that is, Major—Ferris. Ever since he came here, in fact."

"Has there been any increase in his purchases since he came?" What that question could have to do with the silliness he had just made up Longarm didn't know. The nice thing about a man like Petrick was that once hooked he would invent a rationale for himself if he thought one was required.

"Yes. Mmm, six or seven months ago he began to purchase more than had been his normal habit, I should say. Yes, six or seven. Shortly before he, uh, resigned his appointment as marshal, in fact."

"And the medication he has been buying?"

"Laudanum for the most part," Petrick said. "On occasion a restorative for the treatment of acid disorders of the stomach. But for the most part simple laudanum. Quite a common treatment for many maladies, of course."

"But in his case consumption, is that right?"

"Is this necess—"

"Just to establish the need for the medication," Longarm said smoothly.

"Yes, I see. Of course." Petrick harrumphed and looked around. "The man does suffer from the effects of consumption, yes."

Longarm smiled. "And you say it was laudanum he purchased? Never paregoric?"

"Never," Petrick said briskly. "Always laudanum. Paregoric is a camphorated substance suitable for the topical relief of teething pains or for the relief of diarrhea in children, you see. Not nearly powerful enough for the major's purposes."

Longarm looked around and then took a turn at the leaning-forward-and-whispering business. "You've cleared it up completely, Mr. Petrick. The situation I referred to? The substance used was paregoric, not laudanum. You've cleared the major's name entirely, sir."

Petrick beamed with pleasure.

"You've been a big help, sir." Longarm pushed his hand forward and give the storekeeper a handshake and a hearty thank you.

"I'm glad to have been of service, Marshal," Petrick said.

Longarm had no doubt that he had just made the man's day with the line of bullshit. And no harm had been done whatsoever.

He touched the brim of his hat and went off in search of breakfast.

Chapter 9

The Southern Colorado Cattlemen's Protective Association had no offices or formal headquarters. It was run by a man named Cornwall. Longarm got directions to Cornwall's Tenbuck Ranch, rented a horse, and headed out there hoping Ferris might have turned up there since he obviously had not come back to Fort Garland.

The Tenbuck—Longarm could not help wondering if the place was named in honor of some mule deer seen on the property when Cornwall first located it, or if perhaps the big-time rancher who ramrodded the SCCPA had a quirky sense of humor about the worth of land and cattle —was south of Fort Garland in the foothills of the Sangre de Cristos. The road ran from Garland to Taos in New Mexico Territory, with a well-marked turnoff to the Tenbuck. Longarm reached the gate to the headquarters spread in the early afternoon.

He had no idea how many square miles of graze Cornwall and his Tenbuck controlled, but the headquarters was set off from the rest of it by a pole-and-rider fence that enclosed not more than four or five sections. Word was that Otis Cornwall was the he-coon of the San Luis, so this little outfit was damn sure not all of it.

The gate was eight or ten miles east of the rutted highway, the land the fence protected close against the choppy foothills. Longarm dismounted to open the gate—not sure how far he should trust the unfamiliar horse—passed through, and refastened the closure.

"That's far enough," a voice called before he could remount.

He looked up to see a man standing on a knob of earth

not fifty yards away. The fellow was trying to hang onto a Winchester carbine with one hand, button his fly with the other, and maintain a dignified appearance all at the same time. He was not bringing it off particularly well. Longarm must have approached while the guard was away from his post relieving himself. Certainly Longarm and the horse would have been in view from the elevation for some time if the guard had been paying attention.

"I'm friendly enough," Longarm said. He was standing with the bulk of the horse between himself and the guard, and just to keep things on the safe side stayed that way without making another attempt to mount.

"I ain't," the guard called. "Turn away."

"How would you like a vacation?" Longarm asked.

"Huh?" The guard looked confused.

"I asked how would you like a month's vacation. Free room and board. Comes with a nice view through some cell bars."

"I don't know what you're talking about."

"You also don't know who you're talking to. I'm a deputy United States marshal, here on official business. Now, d'you want to discuss this further, or watch while I put some irons on your wrists?"

"Damn good trick if you can do it."

Longarm did not bother to answer that foolishness. There wasn't any doubt in his mind about *could do*. It was only the *would do* that was in question here.

He pulled out a cheroot and lit it, giving the guard time to think it over.

"Well, hell," the man said finally. He rested the butt of the Winchester on the ground.

Longarm swung into his saddle and rode up the knob to face the man. "Interesting that Cornwall keeps a guard on this gate," he observed.

"Mr. Cornwall has enemies," the guard said sullenly.

"So I gather." Longarm eyed the man and was not impressed. He was no gunslick, that was sure. And obviously he wasn't much of a guard, either. Still, that was Cornwall's problem. "Do you want to ride with me to the headquarters?" He hesitated, then said the hell with this guy. "Or would you rather stay here and play doorman?"

The guard flushed a bright red but said nothing. Since he hadn't offered to go along and hold Longarm's hand, the tall deputy kneed the horse forward, outwardly ignoring the guard behind him. He did, however, listen damn close for the sound of a weapon being cocked behind his back. There was none, and he rode on unmolested.

The Tenbuck headquarters was impressive, even if its guard was not. The house was bigger than many hotels Longarm had seen, built of huge logs and two stories high. A broad covered porch extended the full length of the front of it, and it was surrounded by half a dozen log outbuildings. A spring-fed creek bubbled out of a narrow gulch behind the big house, collected in a pond in front of it, and ran off toward the valley to the west.

Two men were busy in a round horse-breaking pen when Longarm rode up. They had a young chestnut gelding snubbed to the well-worn post in the center of the pen. One of the cowboys held a piece of mattress ticking over the gelding's head as a blindfold while the other was trying to cinch a battered breaking saddle in place around the animal's barrel. Despite the blindfold and a heavy halter, the horse was squealing and raising hell with them.

"Nice-looking animal," Longarm said.

The two men hadn't seen him arrive. The one with the blindfold jumped, losing his grip on the cloth and allowing it to slip free of the gelding's eyes. The horse reared back as far as the snub rope would let it and slashed at the second man with its forefeet. Both men had to scramble to keep from being brained.

"Damn, mister. We just about had the son of a bitch. Now look what you done."

"Sorry about that." Longarm dismounted and tied his horse to the top rail of the round pen. There was an easier way to go about that job, but the reception he had gotten at the Tenbuck so far did not make him inclined to demonstrate it for them. The Tenbuck could work out its own problems. "Mind telling me where I can find Otis Cornwell?"

"You the new shooter?" Both cowboys apparently had decided this would be a good time to take a break. They stripped off their gloves and moved to the fence opposite the visitor, leaving the gelding to work out its frustrations at the end of the stout rope.

Longarm raised an eyebrow. "Shooter?"

The cowboy who had been silent gave the speaker a look of warning.

"Billiards shooter," the second man said quickly. "There's a new hand due in, and we heard he's good with a cue. Are, uh, you him?"

Longarm had to give the man credit for effort. He kept a straight face and assured the two that he was not the new billiards shooter on the spread.

"I was just askin'," the first one said.

"Sure. Now about Cornwall . . .?"

"He should be up at the house."

"Thanks." Longarm left the horse where it was and walked the seventy yards or so to the big house. The place looked even bigger the closer he got to it. The porch alone was twice the size of most homes. Rocking chairs had been set out for quiet evenings, and there were several cots at the far end where a man might want to sleep in the cool during hot summer nights.

Nice, Longarm thought.

The door was opened before he could reach it to knock. A fat Mexican woman with a dish towel in her hands asked what he wanted.

"I'd like to see Mr. Cornwall, please."

"Mister Otis is busy now. You write him a letter. Maybe he will see you." She started to swing the door closed in his face.

"Ma'am," Longarm said politely. He removed his hat and smiled. But as he did so he shifted forward far enough to place his boot in the jamb so she could not shut the door. "I've come a long way already, and I really don't have time to play games with Mr. Cornwall. Please tell him he has a visitor. And I *will* see him today, or when I come back it'll be with a search warrant and maybe a troop of cavalry."

"No habla, Anglaise," the fat woman said.

Longarm laughed. "Sure. No better'n I do, anyway. Just tell the man. Please. I'll wait right here."

"What is it you want with your search warrant here, mister?"

"Just a few words. Now if you would be so kind as to—"

"What the hell is all the racket?" The voice was big and booming. It came from behind the woman. She frowned and again tried to close the door, but Longarm's foot was still in the way.

"Cornwall? This is Deputy U.S. Marshal Custis Long. I need to talk with you."

"Well, don't stand at the door shouting, dammit, come inside where I can see you," Cornwall shouted.

The dragon at the door gave Longarm a look like she wanted to spit, but she stepped away and allowed him inside.

Otis Cornwall was a surprise. His voice and reputation were large, but the man Longarm saw at the entrance to a room off the foyer was thin and frail. He was sitting in a high-backed wheelchair with a light lap robe covering wasted legs.

"You're Cornwall?"

"Since the day I was born. You're the one they call Longarm?"

"That's right."

In spite of the reception everyone else around here seemed to be giving out to strangers, Cornwall looked pleased. He wheeled his chair briskly forward and extended a hand for Longarm to shake. "I've heard about you," he said. "Heard you do good work. Even thought about trying to hire you away from the public trough you been sucking at, but my friends in Denver tell me it'd be a waste of postage writing to you. Maybe I was wrong to take their advice?"

48

"You weren't wrong," Longarm said with a smile. "Not that I'm not flattered by the thought."

"Good," Cornwall declared in a voice that was little softer than a bellow. "Good on two counts. I hate waste, dammit. Glad I was right about that. And glad too that you're pleased I thought about you. It never hurts to butter up a man with connections in high places." He laughed heartily. "Now, I know you didn't come here to cause trouble. Everybody says you're fairer than most, and I haven't done anything to earn trouble. So you come inside and have a drink while you tell me what brings you all the way down to this lonesome country." He wheeled his chair around and bellowed, "Consuela," even though the woman was already standing virtually at his side. "Bring us a bottle and two glasses."

"Two glasses, Mister Otis."

"Two glasses, dammit, or I'll fire your ass and send you packing back down to Taos where you belong."

She gave him a disapproving frown but hurried away looking not at all worried that her job was in danger.

"Damned doctors," Cornwall complained as he whisked the rubber-tired chair into a paneled library with more books on its shelves than most public libraries could boast. "Sons of bitches get out of hand trying to order people around. They get their pleasure from denying pleasures to honest people. I'm convinced of the truth of that. Sit down. No, dammit, not there. Take that chair. It's more comfortable. Put your feet up on the hassock there. That's better."

Longarm smiled and set his hat on the floor beside the deep, leather-covered armchair.

"Now. What the hell can I do for you? No. Wait a minute. Just a minute till we get comfortable."

The housekeeper was already back, wheeling a table that held an assortment of bottles and a silver tray with two crystal glasses on it.

"What will you have, Longarm?" Cornwall asked in his overloud voice.

"Rye if you have it, sir."

"Sir? Sir? Did you hear that, Consuela? Since when did I grow old enough to be called *sir* by young pups like you? Call me Otis, Longarm. And I'll call you what I damn please, right?" He laughed again and waved toward the cart. "Rye whiskey for our guest, Consuela, and you know what I want."

She frowned again but poured both drinks: an exceptionally smooth and mellow rye for Longarm, and a colorless fluid for Cornwall that looked like water but quite certainly was not. Longarm decided it would probably be impolite to question the origin of the white whiskey, as the stuff very likely violated federal tax laws.

"To your health, Longarm." Cornwall raised his glass in salute and drank off half his liquor at a gulp. Consuela automatically refilled the glass for him, wheeled the cart to where he could reach it himself if he wanted more, and quietly left the room, drawing the sliding doors closed behind her.

"Now, Longarm, what can I do for you?"

Chapter 10

The simple truth was that Otis Cornwall was a *likable* old son of a bitch.

The man headed a pack of range detectives who were little more than quasi-legal murderers. But Longarm found himself liking the old man anyway.

Before Longarm could get down to the business that had brought him here, Cornwall held a finger up asking him to wait, spun his chair closer to the wall, and gave a tug on a tasseled bell cord.

The housekeeper appeared a moment later, and Cornwall said, "We'll be having a guest for dinner tonight, Consuela, and I want you to make up the north bedroom with fresh sheets. Marshal Long will be staying the night also."

"But . . ."

"No, I won't hear otherwise, Longarm. I know how far it is back to Fort Garland. And no one in his right mind would turn down one of Consuela's special-company meals." He chuckled. "But don't let the old bat know I said so." The woman was standing beside him at the time. She rolled her eyes, shook her head, and marched out of the room. "Now, sir. What is it that brings the pleasure of your company to our table?"

"I need to talk to a man named Tom Ferris. I was told he is one of your, uh, employees."

"Of course. Good man, Ferris. He used to be a major in the army, you know. Resigned his commission and came west for reasons of health. He was town marshal at Fort Garland for a time. Then I was fortunate enough to obtain his services."

51

"After he was fired as town marshal," Longarm observed.

"Resigned, actually."

"By request."

Cornwall shrugged. "A good man nonetheless. Might I ask the nature of your business with Tom?"

"Would it make a difference in how you answer me, Otis?"

Cornwall threw his head back and laughed. "Lord, no, Longarm. An old busybody's curiosity, that's all. Forgive me." In spite of that disclaimer, though, Longarm noticed that Cornwall made no immediate effort to offer information on Ferris.

"I'm not in the habit of discussing government business freely," Longarm said, "but I can assure you of two things. One, I have no warrant for Tom Ferris's arrest." Technically speaking, that was quite correct. One had been issued by now, of course, but Longarm did not yet have it in his possession; it should be in Fort Garland by now waiting for him at the stage company office there. "The other is that what I have to ask Ferris about has nothing to do with the Southern Colorado Cattlemen's Protective Association." He smiled. "Which I suspect is what you are really asking."

Cornwall laughed again. "I had no fear about that, my friend. Our people are instructed to adhere rigidly to all laws and to cooperate with peace officers at all times."

Longarm was not sure if he ought to feel amused or pissed off by that bundle of horseshit. 'Adhere rigidly,' indeed. The so-called range detectives were well known for their habit of shooting from ambush. The rationale apparently was that it saved the taxpaying cattlemen the expense of trials and lawyers. A public service, to be sure.

"If you say so, Otis."

Cornwall spread his palms wide in a show of innocence and smiled. "But I haven't answered your question yet. Tom is not here at the moment. I do, however, know where you can find him."

Longarm sat up straighter in his chair, his interest quickened. "Where?"

"I— Just a moment. I want to give this to you accurately. Follow me, please, Longarm."

The old man wheeled his chair toward the sliding doors, and Longarm hurried to open them ahead of him.

They went out into the hall and toward the back of the house to a masculine study with high ceilings and dark paneling.

"This shouldn't take me but a minute." Cornwall wheeled himself to a huge rolltop desk and slid the cover open. He rummaged through the pigeonholes built into the back of it until with a grunt of satisfaction he produced a slip of yellow paper. "Here. You can read it for yourself."

The paper was a telegraph message form addressed to Cornwall as president of the SCCPA. It read: LUNGS WORSE STOP WILL TRY NEW THERAPY METHOD STOP FORWARD ALL MONIES OWING TO HENSCHER SANATORIUM COMMA MONUMENT COMMA COLORADO STOP WILL ADVISE SOONEST RETURN STOP SIGNED FERRIS

"I couldn't remember the name of the place," Cornwall apologized.

"When did this come in?" Longarm asked.

"Oh, let me see now. Five days ago? It might have been six. Is it important? I could ask Consuela."

Longarm shook his head. "Where was Ferris, uh, working recently?"

"He was making some investigations over on the Picketwire," Cornwall said. "I'm not sure of the exact location."

"That isn't important either," Longarm said.

"Good. We do try to be careful about observing the laws, you know."

Longarm was thinking. Cornwall's information certainly fit. Picketwire was a common name for the Purgatory, or Purgatoire, River, in southeastern Colorado. Over on the other side of Trinidad. A man riding out of that country would probably make for the railroad at Trinidad if he wanted to take the rails north to Monument between Denver and Colorado Springs.

And apparently there really wasn't any connection between the murders in Trinidad and Ferris's SCCPA duties. At least Longarm had not heard about any unexplained deaths in that part of the country. He made a mental note to ask Sam Tevis about that the next chance he got, though, just to be sure.

Longarm glanced at the telegram again, and noticing the reference to the pay due Ferris, idly asked, "What bounty do you pay, Otis?"

The old man's expression clouded over, and he gripped the arms of his wheelchair until his knuckles turned white. "Don't you *ever* call what we do a bounty, damn you."

Longarm stared at the man, shocked by the abrupt change that had come over Otis Cornwall.

"D'you hear me, damn you?" Cornwall shouted. "Do you see this?" He pointed down toward his own useless legs beneath the lap robe. "Do you see what those bastards did to me, Long? They're vermin. All of them. Worse than vermin. They're like rattlesnakes. You clean out a nest of them this year, then next year there's a whole new nest of the vicious, stinking things in the same damn place. So don't you come into my home and talk to me about bounties like we are doing something wrong. We have every right to protect ourselves, by God, and that is exactly what we do and what we will keep on doing."

The old man was shaking from the force of his sudden anger. His voice rose higher and louder until he was screaming the words, and spittle was flying off his lips with every harsh exhalation.

The housekeeper rushed into the study with a glass of some cloudy liquid and a vial of smelling salts. She held him by the shoulders and tried to calm him down.

What the *hell* had he done to bring all this on? Longarm honestly did not know.

Consuela gave Longarm a warning look and motioned with her chin toward the door.

He nodded and left the room as unobtrusively as he

could. Behind him Otis Cornwall was still ranting, his argument lapsing now into incoherent curses.

Longarm shook his head. He hadn't meant to cause an uproar, and still did not believe he had said anything that reasonably should have brought about such an explosion.

Damnation anyway!

The shrieking at the other end of the hall subsided into a babble that rose and fell in volume with the regularity of waves lapping onto a Gulf beach.

Otis Cornwall was mad as a hatter, Longarm realized with something of a jolt.

The old man was stark, raving looney.

Smiling, friendly, likable, hospitable, gracious . . . and crazy as hell.

And until he went off the deep end just then, Longarm had not suspected it for a moment.

Longarm shuddered and went back to the library to retrieve his hat.

He waited patiently in the foyer until Cornwall quieted down. Shortly afterward Consuela slipped out into the hallway.

Longarm soft-footed it down the hall toward her with a finger pressed to his lips. "I . . . please tell Mr. Cornwall that I expressed my regrets, Consuela, but I won't be able to accept his invitation to dinner and a room for the night."

The woman gave him a sad-eyed nod. "It is . . . you come back again sometime, Mr. Longarm. Mister Otis won't remember any of this. He likes you. It would be good for him if you come back again and visit. Okay?"

"Okay," he lied. "When I have time. . . ." His voice trailed away into silence.

He would not be returning to this house of lunacy unless he had to come again on official business. Like to place the old man in cuffs for his own protection as much as for that of the people he hired killed.

Consuela looked at him closely for a moment, then nodded, accepting the surface of the fiction for the sake of politeness. "You come again, Mr. Longarm. I will tell him when . . ." Her smile was very small and apologetic. "I will tell him later."

"Thank you, Consuela."

Longarm jammed his Stetson onto his head and got the hell out of there.

Chapter 11

It was well past dark by the time Longarm got back to Fort Garland. The hostler at the one livery in town gave him hell for being out so late with the horse and making him wait up for Longarm's return.

Longarm accepted the tongue-lashing calmly, paid the man, and walked back toward the hotel.

He had to pass the stage office on his way. The place was closed for the night, the glass in the front windows reflecting light from a saloonfront across the street, but contributing no light of its own. Longarm hoped the warrant he was expecting had come on today's westbound coach. He could inquire about that tomorrow, though. He would have to come to the office to get passage on the eastbound back to the rails anyway.

What he was hoping, actually, was that he would bump into Lisa Howard again this evening. He went so far as to look across the street to her father's hardware store, but the place was as dark as the stage office. Even if he had known where the Howard family lived he would not have called on the girl there.

He was thinking about Lisa—the memory of her bringing an unwanted rise behind the fly of his trousers—as he was passing one of the saloons.

"Marshal Long."

He stopped. It was Lisa's father who was standing at the door of the saloon.

Longarm felt an impulse of guilt that was not at all common for him. But, after all, dammit, he had spent much of the previous night thoroughly romping this man's eldest daughter, and at that very moment was wishing he

57

could do it again. He hoped the light on the sidewalk was not bright enough to show a blush in his cheeks, because he was certain he could feel some warmth there.

"Join me for a drink, Marshal?" Howard was smiling and quite obviously had no inkling about his daughter's favorite pastimes.

"Thanks," Longarm said. His embarrassment was growing, and it was not until the word was already out of his mouth that he realized he did not need an excuse to refuse the offer of a drink. It was only his own stupid guilt that had made him accept with the immediate but erroneous thought that the hardware dealer might suspect something if he went on to the hotel.

Still, done was done. Longarm let Howard lead him inside and set him up with a beer. Breakfast was a long time gone, so he helped himself liberally to the free lunch spread too.

"Still looking for Ferris?"

Longarm nodded.

"He isn't in town. I made sure of that myself. Think I told you already how the son of a bitch was sniffing around my girl Ellie."

"Ellie?" Longarm blurted.

"That's right. Ellie. She's my second oldest."

"I heard someone mention something about a daughter of yours, something about her doing a favor for a shut-in, I believe, but I thought they said her name was Lisa."

"Lisa's my oldest," Howard said. "Wonderful girl, too. Not hard to handle like her sister. But it was the second oldest that damned Ferris was chasing."

Longarm almost felt admiration for randy Major Ferris. Apparently the guy was screwing at least two of Howard's daughters. Hell, maybe he was tapping the mother, too. Or other sisters, if there were any.

The man did seem to get around.

"You might look for him out at the Tenbuck," Howard suggested, unaware of Longarm's line of thought and intent on being helpful if there was any chance it might bring discomfort or worse to Tom Ferris.

"I've just been out there," Longarm said.

"You didn't find him?"

Longarm shook his head. He saw no point in volunteering information on what he did learn there. "That reminds me," he said. "I meant to ask how the Tenbuck got its name. You wouldn't know, would you?"

"Sure. Everybody around here knows that one. Seems old Otis Cornwall came in here, oh, years and years ago, it was. Not too awful long after the U.S. took control of this country from the Mex'cans. He hit the San Louie with ten bucks in his pocket, but he had a good horse and a long rope"—Howard winked—"if you know what I mean. Found the start of a cow herd wandering loose down toward Pueblo, but the next thing you know there wasn't a Mexican brand anywhere in this end of the valley." The man chuckled. "Word is that old Otis still has his ten bucks, too."

Longarm smiled, but the expression went no deeper than the surface of his skin.

It was damned interesting, he thought, that now Otis Cornwall was paying hired gunmen to kill homesteaders for less than Otis himself had done in his youth.

Longarm supposed that the big difference was point of view. *Every* son of a bitch believes whatever *he* does is right.

The biggest pity of the whole thing, perhaps, at least from Longarm's point of view, was that plain old everyday murder was not a federal offense. Without some form of jurisdictional handle, if nothing else a request for assistance from local authorities, Longarm was not allowed to so much as care who killed whom down here in the San Luis Valley.

"Something else I was curious about," Longarm said.

"What's that?"

"What happened to Cornwall to put him in that wheelchair?"

"That happened seven, eight years ago. He was already big by then. Hanging onto his fair share, the way he put it. Hogging everything that was his and twice that amount that wasn't was the way some other parties saw it. Anyway, there was a dispute over some little no-account valley where there was a little water running through, and Cornwall and this other fellow got into a spitting contest over it. Suits and counter-suits and like that. The lawyers were having a helluva fine time of it all. Then one day Otis and his missus were out riding in a buggy. They packed a box lunch and drove down in the direction of this valley Otis was suit-crazy over.

"Well, that night they never came back to the Tenbuck. Next morning his hands went out to look for the two of them. Found the buggy overturned and both Otis and his wife shot in the back. The lady was dead, cold as a trout. Otis lived, but he hasn't felt his toes since. Nobody ever found out for sure who did the deed. They were shot from behind, from ambush."

"And the man who was contesting the land ownership?" Longarm felt sure he already knew the answer to that one.

"They say he decided to pull out in the dead of night. And nobody has ever proven different. Wasn't ever any body found."

Longarm nodded.

The old man was crazy now. Kill-crazy too, possibly. But the sad truth was that there are two sides to every coin, and the world is ever a damn sight more gray than it is conveniently black and white.

Maybe poor looney Otis had some weight on his side of the argument too, even if it was carried too far these days.

Longarm sighed and finished his beer.

"It's been a long day," he said. "Thanks for the drink, Mr. Howard."

"My pleasure, Marshal." Howard smiled. "If you're ever in the market for some bob wire . . ."

Longarm laughed. "When that day comes, I'll look you up. It's a promise."

He walked back to a lonely bed at Fort Garland's one hotel.

He was able to go to sleep without thinking about Lisa Howard or her sister Ellie. Or at least not much.

Chapter 12

The northbound Denver and Rio Grande mixed passenger and freight deposited Longarm at the Monument station shortly after noon two days later. The stage from Fort Garland back to Walsenburg put him back to the rails too late for the last northbound that night. The delay was not so worrisome, though, if Major Tom Ferris was indeed at the sanatorium. And now he had a warrant in his coat pocket made out with Ferris's name on it.

Monument had not changed since the last time Longarm stopped there. It was basically a small railroad town that also did a little business serving nearby farms and ranches.

Trains going in both directions had to stop at the Monument siding to add or remove the extra steam engines necessary for the trains to make the Monument Hill grade north of the town. There was also considerable traffic through the town en route to nearby Palmer Lake. In summer the D.&R.G. ran specials down from Denver for picnickers wanting to take the air or bathe or fish. The lake was several thousand feet higher, and therefore considerably cooler than Denver's sometimes sweltering summer days, adding to the attractions of the resort.

Longarm deposited his gear at the depot. If Ferris was at the sanatorium, he should be able to place the man under arrest and be back in time to make the last train north.

In the meantime he decided to kill two birds with a single stone and get directions to the Henscher Sanatorium while he was having lunch.

Force of habit pointed his boots toward a café he had frequented several times in the past. Some time ago he had known a girl who worked there—had known her delightfully well, in fact—but the last time he was there he learned that she had married and moved away. Today he was only looking for a meal, anyway, and the food there was consistently good.

The plump woman waiting tables at the place remembered him well enough to call him by name when she greeted him. She brought him coffee without waiting to be asked.

"Thanks."

"Are you eating?"

He nodded.

"You'll want the stew. It's extra good today."

"I'll take that, then, and some directions if you can give them." He told her what he needed.

"Oh, my, yes. I know about that place. Everyone around here does. It's the biggest thing around here since the railroad came through." She winked at him. "And until the railroad came there wasn't *any*thing here."

"That big?"

"Gracious, yes. Dr. Henscher is a scientist, you know. He has his hospital up there, and he is conducting research, too. It's really quite something. And of course he employs a lot of people locally. His coming has been terribly good for our economy. I daresay there isn't a person in Monument who doesn't bless the day Dr. Henscher decided to locate here."

"I'm glad for you," Longarm said. He meant it. The people here always seemed exceptionally pleasant, and he was happy for their good fortune.

"Easiest thing in the world to get up there," she said. "You take the old road west and south, then turn onto a new road that angles west. You'll find it just a half mile or so outside of town. It goes up onto Mount Herman. That's where the doctor built his hospital. You can't miss it."

Longarm was habitually skeptical of any directions he couldn't miss, but perhaps in this case it would turn out to be true.

"I take it it's far enough that I'll need a horse or rig to get there."

"Unless you're a fool for walking, I should think so."

"Thanks."

"I'll be right back with your stew."

She was as good as her word, returning almost immediately with a fragrantly steaming bowl of beef stew rich with gravy and tender meat. Longarm was glad he had accepted her advice.

Afterward he checked his watch and walked down to the livery to hire a rig. A horse would have been more convenient, but he would be transporting a prisoner on his way back, and if Ferris was sick enough to check himself into a sanatorium, he likely was too sick to comfortably ride.

The hostler at the livery remembered him also and picked out his best light harness-horse for Longarm to use. Unlike the last time Longarm had been here, the man offered no objection when he was given a government voucher for payment.

"Good to see you again, Marshal."

"Nice to see you again too." Longarm searched quickly through his memory, but if the man had ever given his name, Longarm no longer remembered it. "I see you still have that miserable black."

The hostler laughed. "Still making money off the son of a bitch too. Or I swear I'd kill the critter."

The last time he was here Longarm had earned the old man's respect by asking for, and then accepting, his advice. Which had been to avoid the immensely handsome black that was a favorite of nearly all his customers, but was a stumble-footed, useless bastard as a saddle horse.

"Every man's entitled to his own damn foolishness," Longarm observed. He pulled out two cheroots and offered one to the hostler, then lit both smokes.

"I'm kinda surprised you'd be wanting a driving rig, Marshal, knowin' how you get along with a decent horse."

"I have to go up to the hospital, and I might have company on the way back."

The hostler's eyes lighted up and he gave Longarm a wink of quick misunderstanding. "Damn pretty nurses up there," he said. "To my mind that's one o' the best things 'bout them people moving in here. O' course, I got to admit they been good for business, too."

"Lots of traffic in and out?"

"You bet. Why, I've even ordered me an ambulance to carry the worst-off cases. Found one being sold surplus out of Fort Robinson. I got a wire just today telling me it'll be delivered on the early southbound tomorra."

"Good for you," Longarm said. "I'm glad you're doing so well."

"Ayuh. Not that I had any complaints before, mind, but a little extra is always nice. Gives me a few more dollars to jingle over at the Red Lantern." The Red Lantern, Longarm remembered, was a whorehouse on the north end of town that catered to railroaders. Or to anyone else with the money to pay. Their trade was based mostly on working men, though, relying little on the fancy traffic down from Denver. He understood in a vague sort of way that there was a much more exclusive, and expensive, house that took care of the rich folks' desires.

"This gelding is light-mouthed," the hostler mentioned as he finished buckling the horse into the bars. "He'll pull strong the whole day long and likely won't work up a sweat just getting up to the hospital."

"Thanks." Longarm climbed onto the padded seat, the spindly rig rocking underfoot as he put his weight onto it. He most definitely preferred riding over driving when he had the choice, but this was not a day for choices in that matter. "I don't expect to be too long."

"Long as you need," the hostler told him. "Your word is all I want, and I expect I got that."

"So you have."

Longarm took up a light contact with the horse's bit and clucked the rig away from the livery.

West and then south and then angle onto the new road west, the lady at the café had said.

Couldn't miss it.

And happily enough, you couldn't.

Chapter 13

The Henscher Sanatorium was one hell of an impressive operation.

Longarm followed the graded gravel road through winding switchbacks high onto the side of Mount Herman to an elevation he guessed must be nine thousand feet or thereabouts. High, dry air was thought to be of benefit to the victims of consumption. Because of that an entire industry had developed in the mountains above Manitou to the south of Monument, and now this Henscher was obviously adopting the same policy in his treatment program.

Well before he came in sight of the hospital building, Longarm was passing the familiar tents, very similar to those he had seen before at Manitou, that housed patients whose disease was in arrest.

The tents were tall conical affairs with peaked roofs and sides that could be rolled high to admit the passage of rejuvenating air, or closed against inclement weather.

Today the sides of most of the tents were rolled, and Longarm could see the interiors. Rugs had been laid over the earth of the floors, and each tent was furnished as handsomely as most houses. Better, in fact, than many middle-class homes, with canopied beds, massive bureaus, plush upholstered sofas, and reading lamps with fancy shades.

The Henscher Sanatorium, he gathered, did not cater to the impoverished.

He passed, he guessed, twenty-five or thirty of the tents arranged on terraces cut into the mountainside and connected by a spiderweb network of footpaths and handrails.

All but two or three of the tents appeared to be occupied. Dr. Henscher was doing a good trade here.

When he finally rolled in sight of the hospital itself he damn near gaped.

He had expected nothing like this.

The place was situated on a nearly level plateau of probably three acres' extent against the mountain. It was a good thing so much land was available, because the hospital was huge.

Three stories tall and built of milled lumber, it was bigger than any private building Longarm knew of in Denver. Including the hospital there.

He judged the building to be a hundred twenty feet long and a good thirty feet deep, the depth accentuated by a covered porch that ran across the full front. Glazed windows, each flanked by sets of louvered shutters, ranked along the second and third floors of the massive structure.

The place was painted a bright, confidence-inspiring white, and the shutters and trim were a cheerful blue.

All in all it was one hell of a setup, and all the more remarkable that it could have been erected here so quickly. Longarm had heard nothing about plans for such a hospital the last time he was in this area. And surely any venture of this scope would have been mentioned by someone.

Here too there was much activity. Rocking chairs on the verandalike porch held perhaps a dozen patients wearing dressing gowns and flannel pajamas, and there was a steady flow of nurses in and out of the main doors. The nurses were mostly young, mostly attractive, and wore blue smocks over white uniforms. Longarm was vaguely aware that a nurse's cap indicated something about her training, but he had no way to interpret the plain white dust caps these girls wore.

He smiled to himself, thinking about what the old hostler had said. Now he understood. They were a handsome bunch of fillies indeed.

In addition to the nurses there were several young, husky, and handsome male attendants who were uniformly dressed in blue trousers and crisp white shirts.

Hell of an operation, Longarm thought.

He parked the rented rig in a circular drive that ran in front of the place, and immediately one of the young men hurried down the stairs to join him.

"Do you need help inside, sir?" The man was in his early twenties and had muscles that bulged his shirtsleeves. He looked fully capable of picking Longarm up and carrying him indoors if that was what was required. Maybe the horse too if there was need for it.

"No, thanks," Longarm said with a smile. "I'm a visitor, not a patient."

"Very good, sir."

The attendant took charge of securing the horse to a hitching post before Longarm could get down and see to that himself.

"You might direct me to Dr. Henscher," Longarm said.

"Of course, sir. Follow me."

The young man took Longarm inside to a counter. Behind it was an office presided over by a middle-aged woman in a nurse's uniform. She wore a frilled, many-layered cap that was quite different from the other nurses'.

"Gentleman here to see Bertram," he said, then nodded to Longarm and went on about his business.

"Perhaps I can help you," the nurse said. She wore a brass, badgelike name tag that identified her as Head Nurse Mrs. Hopkins.

"Please," Longarm said. "I'd like to see Dr. Henscher."

"If it is a question about patient admissions or bed availability, sir, I am sure I can . . ."

Longarm pulled his wallet out and opened it to display his badge.

"Oh, dear." Head Nurse Hopkins stared gravely down at the credentials. "I'm sure I don't know . . ."

"It isn't anything to be alarmed about," Longarm assured her. "Now, if I could see Dr. Henscher . . . ?"

The woman recovered her aplomb and gave him a meaningless professional smile. "Yes, uh, I'll have to ask."

Longarm raised an eyebrow.

"The doctor is in his laboratory. He is *never* disturbed

when he is working, Marshal Long. We simply do not do that."

"If you would just take me to him. . . ."

"Oh, no. Gracious, I couldn't possibly do that. No one is ever permitted in the laboratory but the doctor himself. No one. I . . ." She plucked at a gold ornament suspended from a ribbon around her neck and opened it. Longarm had assumed the thing was a locket. Instead, it was a small, stem-wound watch that she consulted. "The doctor should be coming down to the dining hall for his coffee soon. If you could wait just a little . . . ?"

"I'll wait," Longarm said, wondering if it might not be better to just ask Nurse Hopkins where he could find Major Tom Ferris, place the man under arrest, and cart the prisoner off while Henscher was still doing whatever it was that he did in his never-ever-disturbed laboratory.

Nurse Hopkins looked relieved. "Would you care for some coffee, Marshal Long? Or juice? You could wait in the dining hall. We have beverages and snacks available throughout the day and evening." She smiled, on more familiar ground now. "A healthful diet, you understand, is part of the treatment for tubercle disorders. Diet, fresh air, and rest."

"Tubercle disorders, ma'am?" The term was unfamiliar.

"More commonly called consumption or the wasting disease, Marshal Long. Dr. Henscher's research indicates that one of the effects displayed in autopsy studies is the presence of minute tubercles, or lesions, on the lungs of consumption patients. That is why we often refer to the disease here as a tubercle disorder." She smiled again, the expression mechanical. Longarm got the impression that this was a lecture she frequently gave to patients or their families. "The doctor is quite close to determining the *cause* of this unfortunate disorder, Marshal." She sounded as proud of the claim as if she herself were responsible for it.

"And that's what he is doing in the laboratory?" Longarm suggested.

"Exactly," Nurse Hopkins said with a beam of pride like

a schoolteacher rewarding a slow pupil's correct answer. "In here, Marshal Long."

She guided him into a dining hall that held many small tables, each with a clean tablecloth and place settings of sterling and crystal. The dining hall of the sanatorium was set up more like an elegant restaurant than an institutional mess. The patients here were pampered indeed, Longarm thought.

"Please help yourself to the refreshments, Marshal. I will tell the doctor you're here as soon as he comes down." She gave him another flicker of smile and was gone.

Longarm shrugged and strolled across the massive room to a long table. An urn of coffee steamed over an oil-fired warmer at one end of the table, and there were pitchers of cold beverages that he guessed were tea, apple juice, and orange juice, and something else a pale, reddish orange color that he could not identify. The other end of the table held pastries and fresh fruits. Glasses and small plates were provided, as were napkins and dessert forks.

At a table near the windows several patients were gathered in conversation, and another table at the far end of the room apparently was a gathering point for staff. Two exceptionally pert and pretty nurses sat there with their caps off and glasses of juice in front of them. A male attendant every bit as husky as the one Longarm had seen outside came in and joined the girls at the table.

Longarm helped himself to a cup of coffee and a doughnut and carried them to a table at a window to wait for the doctor's convenience.

Chapter 14

Longarm's idea of what a physician and scientist should be was something on the order of a meek, intense little man with a bald head, stooped back, and thick-lensed spectacles, the sort of person who would retreat from the world into the isolation of a laboratory and hide there amid strange experiments and stranger equipment.

Bertram Henscher was not exactly like that.

Longarm was just finishing his coffee when another husky, handsome young man dressed in blue trousers and a white shirt came into the dining hall, stopped to exchange a few words with the pretty nurses in the corner table, and then crossed the room to Longarm.

"Is the doctor finally available?" Longarm asked.

The man grinned and extended a hand. "Yes, I am. Sorry to have kept you waiting."

"You're . . . ?"

Henscher's grin got wider. He was obviously enjoying Longarm's error. Probably it was one that happened often.

The doctor-scientist was probably thirty years old. He had a thick shock of black, curly hair, a tanned face with a square jaw and ruggedly handsome features. And as much muscle padding his shoulders as a strongman in a traveling circus. He was nearly as tall as Longarm and much more solidly built.

Henscher laughed loudly, and Longarm smiled with him.

"Sorry," Henscher said again. "This happens all the time. I have to admit I get a kick out of it." He chuckled. "Some people look down their noses and start giving orders because they think I'm a hospital attendant. When they

70

learn the truth they get so embarrassed they get mad about it. I'm glad you aren't mad at me, Marshal."

The two men shook hands. Henscher's grip was controlled and gentle. The doctor was obviously a man who knew his own strength and felt no need to prove it.

"The apologies have to be mine, Doctor," Longarm told him. "By now I ought to know better than to make assumptions about people."

"We are all guilty of that, Marshal. Mind if I have coffee while we talk? Can I bring you a refill?"

Henscher brought two cups back to the table and sat. "Now, sir. Nurse Hopkins said you need to see me about something?"

"I understand you have a patient here, a Major Tom Ferris from Fort Garland."

A deep and sympathetic concern registered in Henscher's brown eyes. "Yes. The major arrived here a few days ago." He shook his head slowly. "I wish he had come to us earlier."

"Problems?" Longarm asked.

Henscher took a sip of his coffee and gave Longarm a level, steady look. "Before I say anything more, Marshal, I think I should inquire if your visit to the major is personal or, um, professional in nature. There are certain questions of ethics involved here. Confidentiality between doctor and patient, you understand."

"Professional, I'm afraid." Longarm pulled the federal warrant from his coat pocket, unfolded it carefully, and laid it before the doctor.

Henscher took a moment to read the document through, then returned it. "I see."

"Is there any reason why I couldn't, or shouldn't, serve this warrant, Doctor?"

"Bertram. Please call me Bertram. Everyone does. As for your question, unfortunately there is reason why that would not be at all possible, Marshal."

"Longarm," he corrected with a smile. "Please call me Longarm. Most everyone does, Bertram."

"Yes. Thank you. As for the major, though, Longarm, I

am afraid the poor man was very nearly out on his feet when he arrived. Frankly, I don't understand how he managed to find his way to us in his condition. He was heavily medicated, of course, so the pain could not have been severe. But even so . . ." Henscher shook his head again. "He collapsed almost as soon as he realized he was in our charge at last. The poor man has been in a coma ever since."

"Unconscious?"

"Totally," Henscher said. "It is frankly debatable whether he will return to consciousness at all. He could well expire without ever returning to his senses."

Longarm frowned.

"Are you familiar with tubercle disorders, Longarm? With what you might commonly call the consumption?"

"Not in any depth, certainly."

Henscher nodded. It was the normal response and what he had anticipated. "Tubercle disorder is truly a wasting disease, Longarm. And very little understood, which is something I am trying very hard to correct via my work here. Major Ferris is now in an advanced state of the disease. As I say, he could very well expire without ever regaining consciousness. On the other hand, it is entirely possible that he may wake up tomorrow morning wanting a good breakfast and a slug of bourbon. Medical science cannot yet tell us which extreme will occur. If either. The patient—in this case Major Ferris, but the same would apply to any patient in a similarly advanced state of deterioration—may achieve virtually any degree of recovery and might even live a relatively normal life for some time to come, although that period of survival would be marked by recurrent lapses and recoveries. Peaks and valleys, so to speak. Ultimately, of course, the disease must prevail. Ultimately, death will occur." He smiled again, the expression weaker this time and sadder. "Unless, that is, I or some researcher like me is able to provide the world with a true cure."

"Forgive me for showing my ignorance here, Doctor— Bertram, I mean—but I thought that's what you people were doing here already. Curing the disease, that is."

"I wish that were so, Longarm. Unfortunately, the best we are able to accomplish at this point is to arrest the disease. Minimize it. Put it into remission on occasion. We know no actual cure."

"And Ferris . . . ?"

Henscher shrugged. "As I say, I have no way to predict what will happen in his case. I can, however, state with certainty that the man cannot be moved so long as he remains in a coma. His life is hanging by the proverbial thread until or unless his own recuperative life forces bring him out of it. If he were to be moved now he would be dead before an ambulance could get him down to Monument. That I am sure of."

"Damn," Longarm said.

"I agree wholeheartedly, Longarm. Damn indeed. I wish I could bring him out of it. I wish I could cure him and everyone who is suffering like him. But I can't. Not yet."

Longarm nodded. "I'd like to see him, of course."

"It will do you no good, Longarm. As I say, the man is in a coma. There is no way you could question him or . . . whatever it is you need to do."

"Uh . . . no disrespect intended, Bertram. Believe me. But I have to, uh . . ."

"Oh. You need to confirm that the man is indeed in a coma? That we are not providing him an excuse to evade the law. Is that it?"

"Actually . . . uh . . . yes. I'm sorry."

"No, no. I should have thought of that myself. I take no offense. None at all."

"Thanks. If you could just ask a nurse to take me to see him, then, I'll be on my way. I'll have to report in and see what my boss wants me to do about this."

"Nonsense," Henscher said. "I'll show you to his room myself." He smiled. "As a matter of fact, you wouldn't be allowed above this floor without me to accompany you. Standing rules. Our in-hospital patients are all under close observation for purposes of my research. We want no

73

disruptions. In particular we want no homegrown remedies brought in by visitors. Things like that can destroy the validity of my research methods, you see. So we allow no visitors above the ground floor. Patients in no danger, of course, are allowed visitation or off-site travel or whatever they feel up to enjoying. But I do enforce strict regulations when it comes to my research patients."

While they talked, Henscher was leading Longarm back into the long hallway to a flight of stairs leading upward. Another of the brawny young attendants was seated in a comfortable chair near the foot of the stairs with a book open in his lap. The attendant was so unobtrusive about it that Longarm might not have recognized him as a guard if the doctor had not already explained the hospital policy.

The young man looked up as they approached.

"The gentleman is with me, Tim," the doctor said.

"Okay, Bertram." Tim went back to his reading, and Longarm followed Henscher up the stairs.

Henscher smiled over his shoulder. "My staff are mostly university students on sabbatical. I pay them well, and as you can see, they usually have time to study while they are here. I wish I'd had a similar opportunity when I was in school."

Apparently the good doctor hadn't noticed, but the guard at the foot of the stairs wasn't studying anatomy. He had been reading a rather racy novel that Longarm knew had much to do with the female body, but nothing to do with medical science.

"Good-looking boys and girls," Longarm observed as they reached the top of the stairs.

"Yes, aren't they? I employ girls out of nursing schools mostly. As for the boys, I must admit to a preference for young men who play on their schools' rugby teams." He laughed. "Rugby is one of my secret passions, I'm afraid. I like to play in the evenings whenever time permits. I say, you don't happen to play, do you?" He sounded hopeful.

"New blood?" Longarm asked dryly.

That drew a loud, unrestrained laugh from the muscular doctor. It could be taken two entirely different ways. A fresh player for the game, of course, but the sport was well known for its rugged bumps and bruises. The sight of fresh blood was common on a rugby field.

"In answer to your question," Longarm continued, "no. I haven't had the pleasure."

"We might have time for a scrum this evening," Henscher said pleasantly.

"Thanks, but I'll have to see what my boss says before I make any plans."

"Pity." The doctor sounded like he meant it.

The second floor of the hospital was laid out with a long hall down the center of the huge building, with rooms ranged along both sides. The staircase to the third floor was at the opposite end from the one they had just come up, and again there was a burly young attendant reading a book near the base of the stairs. They did not come close enough to him for Longarm to see what this rugby-playing student was studying, but the volume was weighty. This one might actually be working on his education. Longarm wondered briefly why anyone would have built the staircases at opposite ends of the building.

"Here," Henscher said. He returned a chart to its hook on an unnumbered door, knocked lightly, and swung the door open for Longarm.

An exceptionally pretty nurse wearing one of the plain dust caps and blue smocks stood as they entered. She was young, perhaps twenty, and had wisps of flaming red hair escaping from beneath her cap. She curtsied to the doctor and stepped aside.

"Longarm, this is Anna O'Dell. Anna is one of our student nurses."

Longarm nodded to the girl and got a shy, dimpled smile in return.

His attention, though, was on the man in the bed that was the dominant piece of furniture in the room.

The man was painfully thin, his complexion waxy and pale. He was clean-shaven, though, and the sheets on the bed were clean and crisp. There was a faint scent of soap and sun-dried cloth in the air of the room.

A window in the back wall had been opened and the light curtains at it pulled wide. A soft breeze was able to pass through the room by way of a transom over the door.

Longarm had never met Tom Ferris, but the man in the bed fit the descriptions Sam Tevis and Lisa Howard had given.

Ferris lay unmoving at the sound of their voices, his breathing shallow and slightly irregular.

"Any recent change?" Henscher asked briskly.

"No, Doctor. Not since I came on duty."

Henscher nodded and looked at a chart that was hung at the foot of the bed. He looked at Longarm and shrugged, then plucked a pencil from his breast pocket and made a brief notation on the chart.

"If the patient wakens, Anna, I want to be informed at once. Personally. All right?"

"Of course, Doctor." She curtsied again.

Henscher turned to Longarm. "If there is any change, Longarm, I'll get word to you immediately. Would that be fair?"

"Absolutely, Bertram. Thank you."

Longarm nodded a good-bye to Anna and followed the doctor back into the hallway.

"I wish I could be of more help," Henscher said.

"Nothing more you could do, Bertram. Tell me, though, do you have a nurse sitting beside every patient day and night?"

"Heavens, no. Unnecessary except in extreme cases like the major's." He glanced at Longarm, paused for a moment, and then went on. "I wouldn't tell this to just anyone, Longarm, but when there is a . . . likelihood of death, such as in this case, I need to be informed immediately if the patient expires. When that happens, as it does regrettably often once this stage has been reached, I want to get them on the table as quickly as possible for internal examination, before there can be any deterioration of the tissues."

"An autopsy, you mean."

"Yes. Ghoulish from a layman's point of view, perhaps, but if there is any chance I can learn from the dead, can make just the smallest advance toward a cure . . ."

"I understand," Longarm said.

They reached the bottom of the stairs—Tim looking up from his risque novel only briefly—and the doctor extended his hand. "It was a pleasure meeting you, Longarm. If there is anything more I can do, please ask."

"I won't know myself what steps to take next until I check in with Denver," Longarm said. "The marshal might want me back on the job elsewhere, or he could tell me to wait and see if Ferris comes out of it. I'll let you know either way."

"And if there is any change, I'll be sure to send word at once."

"I'll let you know where," Longarm said.

Longarm shook hands with the doctor again and left, nodding a good-bye to Head Nurse Hopkins on his way out. One of the young rugby players jumped to help him reclaim the rig, even though Longarm was entirely capable of doing it himself.

Damned efficient bunch here, Longarm thought as he drove back down to town.

Chapter 15

Longarm drove immediately to the railroad depot and got his wire off to Billy Vail explaining the situation with Ferris and asking for instructions.

It was already late afternoon, though—what with the time it had taken to drive to and from the Henscher Sanatorium and the wait for the doctor while he was there—and there was a good chance Billy would not respond to his request for instructions before morning.

Longarm claimed his luggage from the depot, turned the rig back in at the livery, and took a room at the working-class hotel near the rail station, where he would be easily available to Marshal Vail and Dr. Henscher alike.

The room was small and crudely furnished, but it was clean and it was cheap. The combination was not a bad one.

Longarm was not hungry after a late lunch and the doughnut he had had up at the hospital, so he killed time with a couple quiet beers in a saloon frequented by railroaders and a few cowboys off nearby ranches.

It was a plain place with neither whores nor gaming tables, just a bar where the beer was good and a few tiny tables where a man could go if he liked to sit while he was doing his drinking. Most of the other customers seemed to know each other at least by sight, and their voices were kept low and pleasant. It was not a place where a man would come looking for trouble, and Longarm liked it.

He stayed there until shortly before the telegraph operator was scheduled to go off duty, then wandered back to the depot.

"Anything in for me?"

"No, sir, not yet. I'll be closing down now, Marshal. There will be a railroad operator receiving train orders, but no other message traffic until morning. Unless it's an emergency, that is."

"No emergency," Longarm said and thanked the man. "I'll stop in again in the morning."

"I'm here by seven," the operator said.

Longarm walked toward the center of town. A gap-toothed youngster on a small dun pony caught his eye, and he motioned the boy closer.

"Would you like to make fifty cents, son?"

The boy's eyes practically popped out of his head, and his grin exposed his gums nearly to the back of his throat. "Fifty cents? Are you kiddin', mister?" A dime was considered a handsome fee for nearly any errand.

"It's a fairly long ride I need you to make, but I think you and that good-looking horse should be able to make it before dark."

The boy grinned again at the compliment to his really rather scruffy little pony. "Me and Johnnyjumpup can do it, mister."

"I'd like you to take a message up to the hospital, son. Do you know where that is?"

"He . . . uh, heck, mister, everybody around here knows where 'tis. It's practic'ly on my way home anyhow."

Longarm gave the boy a half-dollar and instructions to let the doctor know where he would be staying at least until tomorrow morning. The kid whistled when he saw the half-cartwheel with Miss Liberty's flowing robes on it. He folded the coin carefully into a bit of cloth that might once have been a bandanna so it would be too bulky to fall through any small holes in his pocket, then put it away with reverent care. Longarm guessed the boy probably had never had so much money of his very own before.

"Anything else you ever need, mister . . ."

"If I do, I'll be sure to let you know, son."

"Thanks, mister. You c'n count on us." Boy and pony wheeled and with a shout of joy thundered out of the streets of Monument in the direction of the sanatorium.

Longarm chuckled as he watched the pair of them go. He wondered if he had ever been that young and enthusiastic about life. Probably not.

He found a restaurant that was considerably fancier than the café where he usually took his meals here, and treated himself to a meal among the swells who were waiting for the last train back to Denver after a day at the lake.

"Good evening, Mr. . . . Longarm, was it?"

Longarm was seated on a bench at the deserted railroad platform, enjoying a cheroot and the evening air. The sun had disappeared some time ago, and now the mountains looming to the west had a dark, almost artificial appearance against a faintly pale sky, looking much like a stage prop cutout.

He stood and removed his hat. "Good evening, Miss O'Dell." It was the nurse who had been watching over Tom Ferris in the hospital room that afternoon. "Did the doctor send you to find me?"

"Sir? Oh." She smiled and shook her head. "It's off duty I am. I came to town to do some shoppin' before the last stores closed." She held up a small package. "I often come here t' sit as I see you've been doin'. I didna mean to disturb you, sir."

"A pleasure, not an interruption," he said. "Would you care to join me?" He smiled. "There's sky enough for us both, I think."

She laughed and took a seat on the bench next to him, fluffing her skirts prettily as she did so. She had changed out of her uniform since he saw her last, and now was wearing a light dress and a shirtwaist that emphasized her figure. It was too dark under the platform roof for him to see the bright color of her hair, but now that the white cap was gone he noticed that she wore the flame-red hair pinned high.

"An odd name, Longarm," she ventured. "I didna believe I've heard the like before."

"It's a nickname," he explained. "Custis Long is the right way around it, Miss O'Dell."

"Then I shall call you Custis if you would call me Anna."

"All right, Anna. Is that Irish brogue I hear in your voice, Anna?"

"Ach, I think not. My old da' was Irish, but I was New York State bred, born an' raised. I've no accent, though now an' again a body thinks I do."

Longarm thought she seriously believed that until he saw the merriment lying deep in her eyes and realized that she was teasing herself and him alike.

"What brought you all the way out here from New York, Anna?"

"Opportunity, o' course. Faint chance of a poor lass puttin' herself through the courses in New York State, Custis. Here I learn more'n most o' those schools could teach me anyways an' get paid for the learnin'. It's the same wi' all o' us. An' it bein' so far away from home, why, who's t' know what all goes on whilst we're away."

"What do you mean, Anna?"

"What? Oh." She turned her eyes toward the darkening mountains. "I meant, o' course, bein' allowed t' come t' town unchaperoned an' like that. 'Twouldna do at all at the straitlaced nursin' schools at home, y' see. Not at all."

She turned back to face him and smiled, meeting his eyes quite boldly now. "There's advantages t' freedoms, y' know," she said. She shifted fractionally closer to him on the hard bench so that he could feel the warmth of her thigh against his.

Longarm smiled, and the girl leaned a bit nearer.

"Cor, you're a han'some lad na, aren't ye?"

Anna raised her face to his, and Longarm found himself kissing her.

Her breath was sweet, and the scent of her was as fresh and clean as the hospital room where she had spent her day.

Her arms crept around him, and she opened her mouth to his kiss, returning it fully.

"You wouldna know a place na quite so public, would ye, Custis?"

"As a matter of fact," he said, "I think I do."

He helped her to her feet and took her hand to guide the way.

Chapter 16

"D'you want the light out?"

"Hell, no, turn it up."

Anna was self-assured and very relaxed. Not at all shy or hesitant. She gave him a coyly kittenish smile and leaned down to turn the wick higher on the bedside lamp.

Longarm closed the bolt on the hotel room door.

The red-haired girl waited until he was watching, then, with the proud, deliberate motions of a burlesque stripper, she began to slowly undo the buttons of her shirtwaist. She dropped it onto the chair and unfastened her dress.

When she stepped out of the garment Longarm whistled softly.

She posed for him, turning from side to side so he could see her to best advantage. He smiled at her.

She wore a garter belt and dark stockings and a light corset that cupped her pale, pink-tipped breasts on shelves of lace and wire.

"D'you think I'm pretty?"

"Silly question."

She gave him another of those small, knowing smiles and reached up to remove the pins from her hair. A quick shake of her head and the hair shimmered down over her pale, soft shoulders like a cascade of fire. She was not wearing drawers under the garter belt. He could see quite easily that the small patch of hair at her crotch was the same flame-red shade.

Anna chuckled at the obvious effect she was having on him and reached behind her to untie the laces of her corset, pulling it free and dropping it with the rest of her things on the chair.

"Very nice," Longarm said.

There was no need to lie about it. Her body was trim, with the sweet elasticity of youth. Her breasts had the size —and the firmness—of demitasse cups, and her nipples were small and pale and sharp-tipped.

Anna laughed and came to him, moving easily into his arms and kissing him hungrily. Her breathing quickened, and her fingers groped between their bodies to find his buttons and release them.

Longarm tried to help, but she shook her head. "Let me. Please."

Ever the gentleman, Longarm did as the lady requested.

She undressed him quickly, taking a moment to linger at the front of his balbriggans when she slid his trousers over his hips.

"Oh, my," she whispered when she saw him. "How lovely."

She ran her hands lightly over his chest and down his belly, dropped to her knees in front of him, and leaned forward to caress his shaft with the softness of her cheek.

"Lovely," she repeated.

"So you are," he said.

Anna brushed his cock teasingly with the tip of her nose and giggled at the response the faint touch drew.

She exhaled slowly, the warmth of her breath tantalizing his sensitive flesh.

"Mmm."

So lightly that at first he was not sure if she was touching him or if the sensation was caused by the heat of her breath, she began to lave his shaft with the tip of her tongue.

Longarm braced himself with his legs wide, and his eyes drooped closed.

"Mmm," she whispered again.

"Uh-huh."

She cupped his balls gently and raised them to her tongue.

"Damn," Longarm groaned.

"You like that?"

"To put it mildly, yes."

His pleasure seemed to please Anna. She laughed lightly and bent to him again. But only for a moment. She stood and took him by the hand, drawing him quite willingly toward the bed.

They lay together, and her slim body was cool and soft to his touch as he ran his hands over her back, then forward, cupping and toying with her breasts and her nipples.

Her nipples had become as hard as rock candy now. And as enjoyable to taste.

He mouthed her, nipping lightly at her with his lips, and Anna moaned and arched her back, raising her hips to him and opening herself wide.

Longarm obliged and found her wet and receptive and as hot as a freshly stoked furnace.

"Don't wait, luv. Take me na, and I'll fetch the lovely thing up again for ye in no time."

Longarm mounted her, and Anna lifted herself to meet and to envelope him.

She clamped herself tight around him with surprisingly strong arms and fiercely demanding legs and clung to him with a surge of joyous energy.

"Ah, yes. So good. So ni' when you fill me this way." She bit down on her full, pouty underlip and thrashed her head from side to side as her own passions grew, swelled beyond containment and overflowed with a gasping, pulsing rush.

Longarm had held back. Now he continued to stroke slowly in and out, in no hurry, letting the girl's senses rest for a moment. Then, with deliberate care, he stepped up the pace, a little at first, then more.

He could feel Anna's responses grow once again as she rose to meet him.

Then, together this time, he bucked and plunged, spearing her with his own superheated flesh. Pummeling and demanding. Slapping his lean belly wetly against hers quicker and quicker until both of them exploded, and his fluids burst out to flood her with his heat.

Anna cried out, her arms and legs convulsing around

him, the lips of her sex contracting in spasms that clenched and stroked him.

She bit sharply into the pad of muscle on his shoulder and then collapsed beneath him, utterly spent by the intensity of her climax.

Longarm smiled and lightly nuzzled the side of her sweat-damp neck. There was no response, and for a moment he was puzzled.

Then he realized that the girl had fainted dead away for the moment.

With another smile he eased himself out of her and let himself down to lie beside her now-warm body.

Anna stirred and opened her eyes. "I know I made ye a promise, luv. But gi' me a minute, will ye?"

Longarm laughed and reached for a cheroot. "We'll take the whole night long if that's what you like."

"Aye," she whispered. "What a lovely thought, that." She rolled to face him, and her breasts lay warm and sweet against his chest.

Chapter 17

Billy Vail's wire was already waiting at the depot when Longarm walked over there after breakfast the next morning. He had eaten more than usual and considerably later thanks to the pleasantly hollow sensation he retained after Anna's visit. He did not envy the girl having to put in a day's work now after being out so late.

He stifled a yawn, pulled out a cheroot, and opened the message form the telegrapher gave him.

ARREST SUSPECT OR CONFIRM DEATH AND RETURN WITH DEATH CERTIFICATE STOP ADVISE PROGRESS IF ANY STOP SIGNED VAIL

Longarm shrugged. Either they were not busy in Denver right now or someone in the army with impressive political connections was demanding results. Either way, he was willing to go along with whatever Billy wanted on this one.

He smiled to himself. It wasn't like he was having such a terrible time of it while he was in Monument.

He tucked the telegraph form away and lit the cheroot, then walked over to the livery.

"You want that rig again today, Marshal?"

"No, I expect I'll be by myself today. A good horse will do me just fine. If you still have that little mare . . . ?"

"Sold her," the hostler said, "but I have a pretty decent little gelding you can use." He chuckled. "Or you could take the black."

"I'll trust your judgment," Longarm said with a smile.

The hostler hurried to saddle the best horse he had for the friendly deputy.

Rather than go back to the hotel to lug his own McClellan over, Longarm accepted the use of a livery stock saddle on the horse. The thing felt bulky and soft after so many years of using a ball-busting military seat, but he had to admit the big rig was comfortable. And he did not expect to be riding far enough or long enough for its much greater weight to be a problem.

"I'll be back after a while," Longarm told the hostler.

"No hurry on my account. Use him like he was your own. I reckon I know you good enough by now t' not worry."

"Thanks."

Longarm bumped the blue roan gelding into an easy road jog through town and then stepped it up to a smooth, rocking-chair canter until he started the climb toward the Henscher Sanatorium. He let the horse walk from there, and it never broke a good sweat. As always, he was pleased with the way the hostler had treated him.

"Good morning." Longarm dismounted and handed his reins to one of the ever-present attendants outside the hospital.

He took the steps two at a time, feeling good in the fresh, clean air of this altitude.

"Morning, Nurse Hopkins."

"Good morning, Marshal Long." The woman was efficient and businesslike. She thumbed through a wire basket of papers, extracted one and read it over. "The doctor left orders that you are to be informed of any changes in Major Ferris's condition, Marshal."

"That was thoughtful of him. And?"

"And what?"

"And has there been any change?"

"Oh." She had to look at the paper a second time. "No. No change as of the change of shift this morning."

"You keep someone in the room with him even at night?"

"Oh, yes. Doctor's orders. If anything, uh, untoward happens, the doctor is to be informed at once. Even if he is in the middle of a scrum."

Longarm got the impression that was just about as serious as disturbing him when he was in his laboratory. The man really loved that game.

"Is the doctor in the lab now?"

Nurse Hopkins checked the watch that hung at her throat. "He should be in the dining hall now. Would you like to see him?"

"If it's convenient."

"I'm sure it would be." She checked the watch again, and this time she smiled.

Nurse Hopkins escorted him down the ground-floor hall to the dining room even though Longarm already knew the way. Bertram Henscher was seated at a pair of tables that had been pulled together. He was surrounded by young men and women in the uniforms of his staff. The bunch of them seemed to be having a good time together. The medical scientist looked little older than the students who worked for him, and he was very much at ease in their company.

"Longarm." He grinned and waved a welcome. "Join us?"

Longarm pulled a chair over from another table and straddled it with his arms resting on its back.

"Coffee?"

"I just had a big breakfast, thanks."

"I'd be glad to get some for you," a plump, pretty blonde nurse offered.

"All right, then. Thank you."

She gave him a baby-doll smile and crossed the long room to the buffet table with her hips swaying right fetchingly. Longarm looked around but there was no sign of Anna this morning. Which was probably just as well. He was not sure how she would want him to act toward her here at the hospital. Too friendly and he might embarrass her. Too formal and it could insult her.

Bertram Henscher laughed and turned to one of the young men seated at the table. "Do you remember the boy who showed up here yesterday evening?"

"The little kid with no front teeth?" The fellow laughed. "I couldn't forget that one."

Henscher turned back to Longarm with a grin. "The little messenger you sent caused quite a stir."

"He did?" The nurse came back to set a cup of coffee and a pair of doughnuts in front of Longarm, and he smiled her a thank you while he listened to the doctor.

"He certainly did. He came tearing up to the porch on that pony of his and jumped off as excited and out of breath as if he'd been a Pony Express rider with the Sioux after him. Charged up the steps and began yelling for me. Ronny here tried to stop him, but the little rascal wouldn't hear of it. He ducked away from Ronny and started running up and down the halls shouting for me." The doctor's laughing was interfering with his ability to tell the story. The young man named Ronny took over for him.

"There was this kid, see, dashing back and forth just as hard as he could run and shouting his head off, and before you know it there was, oh, a half dozen of us chasing him, I guess, and wondering what it was all about. Finally Bertram heard the commotion and came downstairs, and we were finally able to capture the little guy and get his story told."

"Let me tell you, Longarm, when you need a message delivered you can count on that boy. He took the job to heart." Henscher's laughter slowed to just chuckling, and he dabbed at his teary eyes with the corner of a handkerchief.

"The little guy had us in an uproar for ten, fifteen minutes, and there weren't enough of us in the whole place, I bet, to catch him until he was ready to be caught."

"Well, I certainly didn't mean to cause you all that trouble. I just wanted to let you know where I'd be."

Henscher grinned and gave the young people at the table a wink. "Do us a favor, Longarm? If you want to tell us something, send up smoke signals or mail us a letter. But please, please *don't* sic that youngster on us again."

"It's a promise," Longarm said.

"Will you be staying in town for a while?" Henscher asked.

"Until something happens with the major, apparently. Until either I arrest the man or see him buried."

Henscher nodded. "We can reach you at the same place?"

"Until I tell you otherwise."

An attendant Longarm recognized from the day before —Tim, he thought the boy's name was—excused himself, and so did several of the girls.

"You gentlemen of leisure can talk all you like," said the pretty blonde who had brought Longarm's coffee, "but us working-class folks have to get busy." She smiled at Longarm and added, "We have a frightfully demanding boss, you know."

Bertram Henscher laughed as loudly as any of them.

"I'm not keeping you from your work, am I?" Longarm asked.

"No. I'll relax a few minutes more, then go back up to the laboratory. When I need to leave, believe me, politeness won't bar me."

The other young nurses and attendants finished their snacks and left, leaving Longarm and Henscher alone at the table.

"They're a fine group," Henscher said with obvious pride.

"So they seem." Longarm took another sip of the coffee. "If you don't mind me mentioning it, you seem rather dedicated yourself, Bertram. Do you mind if I ask why?"

Henscher's expression became serious for the first time since Longarm arrived.

"I must admit to having an intense personal interest in the battle against tubercle disorders, my friend," he said. "Consumption took my grandfather when I was very young. And while I was still in school it claimed my mother also. At the time, actually, I was studying business law. Had no intention of going into medicine. The shock of her passing was . . . devastating. I dropped out of school, even came quite close to becoming a drunk. But I got hold of myself, went back to school." He spread his hands and smiled. "You see the result here. I would do anything, Longarm, literally *any*thing, to defeat this disease that has cost me so much."

"Your father must be very proud of you, Bertram," Longarm said.

"What?"

"Your father. I mean, the way you have dedicated yourself to finding a cure for the disease that took your mother."

"Yes. I'm sure. Except that I never knew my father. He abandoned my mother and me when I was just an infant. My grandfather and mother were the only family I ever knew. Tubercle disorder took both of them. *All* my family."

"Rough," Longarm sympathized.

Henscher shrugged. "Worthwhile, perhaps. If I succeed."

"I hope you do, Bertram. I truly hope you do."

"If you would excuse me now, Longarm. I must get back to my work."

"Of course. Thanks for the coffee. And for the help."

"If anything changes, of course, I shall send word down to you immediately."

"Thanks, Bertram. Oh. It might be good if I could stop in now and then and take a look at Ferris. Would that be a problem?"

"Not at all. Do you want to see him now?"

"No, I don't think so. I don't want to keep you from your lab any longer. Just now and then will be fine." He smiled. "Besides, that gives me an excuse to come up occasionally and visit. You and your people are enjoyable to be with. And a peace officer can't often say that about the folks he deals with day in and day out."

Henscher laughed and extended his hand. "Next time come in the late afternoon," he suggested. "You can stay for dinner, and I'll try to talk you into joining one of our games." He patted his stomach. "Good for you, you know."

"The eating part I'm willing to take on. The rest... we'll see."

They shook hands good-bye, and Longarm found his own way out past Nurse Hopkins's station.

Chapter 18

The view from the road on Mount Herman was exceptional. Behind him rose the ragged bulk of the Front Range. In front of him was the start of the Great Plains, sweeping virtually unbroken across Colorado and Kansas and on into Missouri. Near the mountains, spread out virtually beneath Longarm's toes as he rode down from the hospital, was a dark mass of rolling, wooded hills with the grasslands stretching for hundreds of miles beyond the clumps of pine forest.

The day was as fine as the view, and Longarm was enjoying it.

He leaned back against the cantle to balance his weight over the horse while the animal tiptoed down the sloping road, its butt shifting widely from side to side and Longarm balancing without conscious thought by reflex.

The horse negotiated yet another of the many switchbacks that were required to make a road level enough to permit wagon and ambulance traffic, and Longarm reached inside his coat for a cheroot. He was thinking about lunch.

Without warning the horse boogered, throwing its head high and trying to rear.

"What the . . ."

Longarm snatched his hand out of his coat pocket and straightened in the stirrups as the horse flung itself backward.

A hollow, booming report sounded only a few yards distant, followed immediately by the wet, ugly slap of lead striking flesh and bone.

The horse became dead weight between Longarm's

knees as a bullet intended for him buried itself in the roan's skull.

Longarm pitched himself sideways, his right boot tangling for an instant in the unfamiliar stirrup of the rented saddle.

The boot slipped free, but it had held him up long enough that his other foot was trapped at the ankle beneath the falling horse.

The half-ton body slid downhill several feet, dragging Longarm's leg with it and scraping his boot across the gravel.

Colt already in hand he kicked, jamming his free foot against the seat of the big stock saddle and shoving with all his strength to drag his boot loose.

A fold of leather caught, held for an instant, and then released.

Longarm came to his knees, .45 leveled.

The ambusher had been lying in wait below the road at the switchback.

Now Longarm could hear the skitter of loose rock as the gunman tried to scramble down the mountainside toward the road below the next switchback.

Longarm jumped up and ran to the edge of the road.

A thick tangle of scrub oak and rock blocked his view of the slope under his feet, but the roadway only twenty-five or thirty yards down was in full view.

The gunman was somewhere on the slope. Longarm could still hear him.

A flicker of movement below brought the muzzle of the big Colt to bear, and Longarm's finger tightened on the trigger.

"Shit." He let off before firing, and a black and white magpie lurched out of the undergrowth to take swooping flight toward the distant plains.

The sounds of sliding gravel ceased, and Longarm dropped to one knee.

If the ambusher tried to bolt across the road he would be exposed against bare soil for long seconds. More than enough time for an aimed shot.

If he tried to creep away through the brush, the sounds of his movement would betray him.

The man had to know that. The son of a bitch would be sweating now, knowing his one chance had failed with that frightened toss of the roan's head. The horse had taken the bullet meant for Longarm. And the gunman's chances with it.

"This is Deputy Marshal Custis Long," Longarm called out in a clear, calm voice. "You can give yourself up and live to see the inside of a courtroom. Or you can take the other way out. Up to you."

He edged sideways for five feet as soon as the sound of his voice had spotted him for the ambusher. Just in case.

There was another flash of motion down below, but this time it was not a magpie's wings.

A head and shoulders came into view from behind a red sandstone boulder.

The man had a stubby carbine in his hands.

He tried to bring the barrel of the weapon in line, but he was aiming well to Longarm's left, at the point where Longarm had been when he spoke.

Longarm's Colt spoke first, the downhill shot an easy one, and a .45-caliber slug smashed into the ambusher's chest just below his throat.

The man flung his arms wide in his death throes, the carbine firing harmlessly toward a puffy cloud high overhead, and he fell backward out of sight behind the boulder.

Longarm dropped back into his crouch and shifted position again. There probably was only the one ambusher. But he was not going to stake his life on that probability.

Again he called out. Probably talking only to the dead. Possibly to a second gunman.

"The offer still holds. Give yourself up. I won't shoot if you show yourself with your hands empty." He moved location again, this time going in the other direction.

There was nothing but silence in response.

He waited. Patience costs nothing. Impetuousness can be fatal.

"Last chance," Longarm called.

And again he waited.

The only sounds that reached him were the distant chirruping of a mountain bluebird and the drone of a bee. Shadow from one of the small clouds floating far above drifted down the mountainside making rapid, odd adjustments in shape as it covered the jagged contours of the earth with patterns of light and dark.

Longarm waited a measured fifteen minutes and then forced himself to sit it out for another ten. Finally he got to his feet. But still he kept the Colt ready in his hand.

Moving slowly and keeping to the side of the road where dry bunchgrass padded the gravel of the soil, he followed the road to the next switchback and on to a patch of white wildflowers that he had noted from above.

The place where the gunman had gone down was only a few yards away.

Longarm could see a spurless boot and blue pant leg lying motionless on the ground.

If the man was still alive he could be lying doggo, wanting one last opportunity to shoot. Longarm had seen a carbine, and it had fallen wide of the boulder behind which the body lay. That did not mean the man had no handgun.

The hell with taking chances.

Longarm cocked the double action Colt to gain the light smooth pull of single-action fire, took careful aim, and blew one into the back of the man's calf.

The exposed leg jerked, but only from the impact of the heavy slug smashing into it.

The ambusher was dead.

And almost certainly alone. No live partner was apt to remain silent and motionless at the unexpected gunfire. If there had been a second man he would surely have reacted.

Longarm eased out into the road, Colt still ready, until he could see the entire scene.

The ambusher was dead, his eyes staring sightlessly toward the sky and blood drying under his head and shoulders from the fatal wound high in his chest.

The man was hatless and had no belt gun. Just the large-bore Sharps carbine he had dropped. Longarm checked the carbine. It was an old military issue breech-loader that had been converted to handle .52-caliber rimfire cartridges.

Longarm shook his head and knelt to examine the man who had tried to kill him.

The dead man looked vaguely familiar. It took Longarm a minute to place him.

His name was Jack. Jack Humphrey? Humphries? One or the other. He was on the Wanted posters, the line-drawing likeness actually pretty good for a change.

If Longarm remembered correctly, this Humphrey or Humphries was wanted for robbery and murder in Wyoming Territory and was on federal warrants for mail theft. Longarm could not recall what the reward on him was—not that it mattered, since Longarm could not collect on it anyway—but he thought the amount was unusually high. Several thousand dollars, anyway. Run-of-the-mill petty crooks generally earned no more than a few hundred dollars on their heads.

No one had to worry about this one any longer. Jack Humphrey was out of the mail robbery business for good.

Longarm cussed a few times and looked around.

The man must have had a horse to get up here, but the damn thing must have run away at the sounds of the shooting, dammit.

It was going to be a long walk back to Monument, particularly carrying that heavy damned stock saddle.

Longarm shook his head. Humphrey must have been breaking back into the rough country behind Mount Herman. Must have seen the federal officer coming down the road practically right on top of him from below that switchback.

It had been shitty luck for both of them.

But somewhat better for Custis Long than for Jack Humphrey. Or Humphries.

Resigned to the inevitable, Longarm hiked back up to the dead roan and with some difficulty pulled the saddle off the thousand pounds of carrion. He would have to leave it for someone else with a horse to provide the muscle to drag the roan out of the roadway.

Just getting himself and the saddle back down to Monument was going to be work enough for this day.

"Damn," he said aloud as he draped the heavy Frazier over his shoulder and started the long, hot walk.

The day did not seem so fine to him as it had.

Chapter 19

The hostler hurried out to meet him and took the saddle onto his fresher shoulder. Longarm was frankly dragging. He wanted a chair and a drink and he wasn't sure which he wanted first. The plain fact was, though, that there was no time for either right now.

"You all right, Marshal?"

"Sure. Thanks." He grinned. "I've always enjoyed walking. But that was ridiculous."

"What happened?"

Longarm explained briefly, and the hostler looked actually relieved.

"I was afraid that damn horse of mine done something it oughtn't. Glad to hear it wasn't him."

"No. The government will pay you what he was worth, of course. You have my word on it."

"That's good enough for me, son."

"There's something you might do for me if you would," Longarm said.

"Name it."

"I'll need to see your town marshal or county sheriff, whichever is handy, to report the shooting."

"Um. Sheriff's down in Colorado City, and we don't have need enough to hire a marshal. There's a deputy lives over to Palmer Lake, though. I could send for him. Done in as you look, why don't I send word that he should meet you at Sawyer's. Have you a beer or two an' you'll be feeling better by the time he gets here."

"I'd appreciate it."

Longarm limped off toward the saloon the hostler had mentioned. His left foot, the one that the horse had fallen

100

on, was aching after the hike. Even so he had come out a damn sight better off than Jack Humphrey had. There was that to be thankful for.

He stopped at the railroad depot to get a wire off to Billy Vail, telling him he could take Humphrey off the Wanted list, and went on to Sawyer's saloon.

Nothing, absolutely nothing, had ever been more welcome or better tasting than that first swallow of cool, throat-drenching beer.

He drank the first one down in a hurry and carried a refill to a vacant table. He was still there an hour later when a slender young man with spectacles and a badge pinned to his vest came in.

"Over here." Longarm motioned the deputy closer and pushed a chair out.

"Marshal Long?"

"That's right." Longarm stood and the two men shook.

"I'm Buddy Wisman. Deputy for this end of the county."

"Thanks for coming, Buddy. I hope I didn't take you away from your dinner."

Wisman grinned. "No, but I reckon I better not say what you *did* call me away from. I, uh, only been married three weeks."

Longarm chuckled.

"Mr. James tells me you got involved in a shooting scrape?"

James. Albert James. That was the hostler's name, by damn. Longarm had forgotten he'd ever heard it. "I'm afraid so." Longarm described the incident for the county deputy, Wisman holding up a finger now and then to slow the flow of the story while he jotted notes into a pad he carried in a breast pocket.

"No problem, of course. I'll write up a report on it and send it in to my boss and a copy to Denver. And Mr. James has already got some fellas to go with him in a wagon to collect this Humphrey fella's body and move the dead horse out of the road. I think that should cover it."

101

"That should be fine, Buddy. I appreciate you going to the trouble."

"It's what we get paid for, right?" Wisman looked through his notes again and asked, "You say this man was riding up the road and apparently seen you coming down it? Likely thought you were after him and decided to shoot first?"

"That's assumption, of course, and not fact. I never found his horse . . . wish to hell I had so I could've ridden it down instead of walking the whole way . . . but it's the only explanation that makes sense. Of course I *wasn't* after him or anybody else, but he wouldn't have known that. The silly part of it is, Buddy, I'd likely have nodded and smiled and ridden right past the man without once thinking about those posters out on him if he hadn't up and started shooting."

"This Humphrey knew you on sight but you didn't know him?"

Longarm shrugged. "A man in our business, we have to show up in courtrooms and jails and on witness stands so damned often there's no telling who'd recognize who. I surely don't remember seeing this Jack Humphrey ever before, certainly never did in the line of duty like when he was in cuffs for anything, but he could've been a spectator in a courtroom someplace or seen me in a bar or hotel. . . . Hell, there's no way to ever know now that the guy is dead."

Wisman grunted. "Seems logical," he said.

"Look, I've forgotten my manners here. Can I buy you a beer, Buddy?"

Wisman grinned. "I got reason t' hurry home now if you don't mind."

"You do that, Buddy. And carry my apologies to your bride. I'll try not to be so rude again," Longarm said with a chuckle.

Buddy Wisman tucked his notepad away and hurried outside.

Longarm noticed that night had fallen while he was in Sawyer's waiting for the deputy. And he never had gotten around to having that lunch he'd been looking forward to.

He shoved his chair back and stood, feeling much better now than he had when he came in.

Good enough, in fact, to wonder if Anna O'Dell would be in town for the evening.

Chapter 20

Anna O'Dell was not in town that evening, or at least Longarm did not see her there, but he encountered her on the sidewalk the next morning as he was leaving the café after breakfast.

"Ma'am." He tipped his hat and received a smile in return.

"Custis." She glanced around to see that they were not overheard. "I've been thinkin' about you, Custis. Ever since the other night. You *do* know how to make a girl feel good."

"I'd have to admit that I was hoping to run into you last night," he said.

"I'm flattered. But I had to work last nigh'." She smiled prettily. "Would it interest you t' know that I'm off today? All day?"

"That does seem to have certain prospects, doesn't it."

"*I* think so." She gave him a coquettish look. "Do ye like t' go on picnics, Custis?"

"Like over to Palmer Lake?"

"Only if ye insist on comp'ny, luv. But as it happens, y'see, I know o' a grand little place where unwelcome strangers ben't likely to stray." She arched her back just a little, not so much that anyone else on the street might notice. But certainly enough for him to see.

Longarm grinned at the forward little wench and whistled softly.

And to think, he was being paid for this duty in Monument.

"Why don't I go make the arrangements," he suggested.

"I'll have a lunch put up and hire a rig, then meet you . . . where?"

"Ye know the big tree on the road t' the 'ospital? I've a bit o' shoppin' t' do. I'll get that done an' meet you at the tree."

Longarm smiled and touched the brim of his Stetson again.

"You'll not be long, luv?"

"Not a minute longer than I have to be," he promised.

"Ah, what a lovely turn o' events for a borin' day," Anna said happily. She walked on down the block, and Longarm went back inside the café to arrange for a boxed dinner they could prepare while he went to hire a buggy.

Instead of turning onto the road that led up Mount Herman, Anna guided him south. The public road branched and narrowed until they were following a thin, seldom-used track that crossed the rolling country beneath the Front Range foothills.

"Cross the crick there an' then turn up," Anna directed.

The livery horse splashed through the thread of water, and Longarm turned it west toward the mountains. Only a few ruts showed that they were not the first people ever to come here. From the valley they followed it was impossible to see any sign of mankind.

Somewhere behind them a train whistled its approach to the Monument depot.

"I do love it here," Anna said with a sigh. "S' wild an' free. Ye'd think we was the only two on airth."

Now that they were out of view from any prying eyes, she moved closer to him on the leather-upholstered seat of the buggy and rested her hand comfortably on the inside of his thigh, then laid her cheek onto his shoulder. She sighed. Her touch, light though it was, held a vivid promise. Longarm held the reins with one hand and slipped his other arm around her.

"Lovely," Anna said.

"And so you are."

She smiled at him.

105

The horse pulled the buggy deeper into the valley.

"That way," Anna said. She pointed to the left, up a tiny thread of water that trickled down from a narrow side valley. "No, cross over first, luv. We don' want t' get hung up."

She had been here before obviously. Longarm felt no resentment. The girl was young and pretty and alone and far from home. She offered no strings and she demanded none.

The buggy bumped across the feeder creek with a jolt, and for several minutes Longarm had to pay attention to his driving until they cleared a screen of scrub oak at the mouth of the miniature valley. Then the foliage thinned and the rig was able to roll free.

"Up almost to the end," Anna said. "I'll show you where."

"Here," she said a few minutes later.

Longarm tended to the horse while Anna took the picnic basket and disappeared behind another screen of low-growing scrub oak with the warning, "Don't follow now, luv. Wait righ' here till I fetch ye."

"I'll wait," he promised.

He took the horse out of the bars and picketed it where it could reach some of the thin, tough bunchgrasses that grew in the meager soil here, then sat on the singletree and smoked a cheroot while he waited for Anna to return. She seemed to be taking more than time enough to lay out a picnic.

"All right, luv. Come down na."

Longarm shrugged and ground the cheroot out under the toe of his boot before he stepped down through the thick oak scrub.

There was no path but he could see where Anna had gone before him, crushing the grass down underfoot as she walked. He trailed behind her, curious now but pleased. The pretty nurse seemed to be enjoying the outing every bit as much as he was. There was excitement in her voice when she called, "Ye're comin', are ye?"

"Right behind you."

She sounded close, but he still could not see her.

He followed her to an ancient, gnarled spruce and had to duck low to pass beneath its branches.

"Damn," he said with pleasure as he straightened.

Hidden between the spruce and a sheer wall perhaps twenty feet high at the southern side of the tiny valley was a glade of jewel-like beauty.

The pocket of flat ground, no more than ten feet square, was carpeted with thick, lush grass of a brilliant emerald color. The grass was fed by a spring that trickled out of the hillside, the dancing water sparkling in the sunlight like diamonds and collecting at the bottom to create the little stream they had followed up here.

Best of all, though, was Anna.

The picnic basket had been set aside untouched.

Anna's time had been spent preparing herself, not a meal.

Her dress was neatly folded and laid next to the basket, as were her shoes and stockings and undergarments.

She had unpinned her hair and let it down.

Longarm had seen her before, of course. But never in the sunlight. Never quite like this.

Sunshine caught and reflected on the wavy flow of her long red hair, the highlights shimmering with every breath and motion, so the sight of it put the diamond gleam of the springwater to shame.

Anna lay on her side in the center of the grassy patch, the color of her hair in exciting contrast with the color of the grass.

Her body was slim and pale and inviting.

She smiled and rolled onto her back, letting her head loll back and her eyes close as she lifted her face to the sun.

Her nipples, so small and sharp-tipped, were a delicate pink that blended into the pale flesh of her firm breasts. Her skin in unshaded daylight was so fine he could see a tracery of blue veins beneath it on the upper slope of her breasts and high on the insides of her thighs.

Longarm felt the quick, eager stirrings of an erection as

107

he looked at what she had prepared for him here.

As of course Anna had damn well intended.

"You *do* know how to picnic, ma'am."

Anna chuckled and held her arms open to him.

Longarm lay beside her, and her mouth opened to his.

Her tongue probed light and teasing between his lips, and he stroked the bright red hair on the side of her head and down over her shoulders, then let his fingertips trail lightly over her right breast, across a taut rib cage and down over her belly.

Anna shuddered and parted her legs to his touch as he twined red curls around his finger, then touched her gently. She was already wet and receptive.

He could hear a quickening in Anna's breathing as he rubbed the tiny bud of her pleasure.

"Oh, Custis. Don't make me scream so soon, lad. I wanta take th' whole day t' enjoy this."

Even as her mouth whispered the denial into his ear, though, Anna was raising her hips to meet his touch, opening herself wider to him. Her body demanding what her lips said should wait a while longer.

Longarm chuckled and nuzzled her nipple while he continued to stroke her softly toward the brink of pleasure.

"We have all day," he agreed. "And we'll use it, Anna. Every minute of it."

He cupped one breast in his hand and squeezed while he continued to suck greedily at the other.

He kneaded and teased at her with the other hand until Anna's hips began to pump, and her breath came quick and shallow to lips that were drawn back over her teeth as the sensations he was creating in that young, slim body built beyond containment.

"Ah. Ah. *Ah!*" Her whole body strained, as taut as a drawn bow, and she arched high off the ground, her legs clamping tight around Longarm's hand as she reached satisfaction and exploded past it. "Custis. *Custis!* Yes!"

The girl's body quivered and strained for long, intense moments.

Then she sank back onto the soft, sweet-smelling grass, spent and limp in temporary satiation.

"But I haven' done a thing for you, luv."

"Not yet," he said with a smile. "But I think there's time enough for that. Don't you?"

"Aye," she said happily. "Any way ye like." She laughed. "Better yit, dear man, *every* way ye like."

"I'll give that some thought," he promised.

"An' I'll give it me all, dear."

Anna rolled onto her side to face him and snuggled tight against him, wrapping her warm naked body close to his. She sighed and tried to wriggle even closer.

"Ach," she said with a note of surprise in her voice. "All this ye've done fer me a'ready an' I've not e'en got the pants off the man yit. What kind o' selfish hussy must ye think me? I'll no' have ye think that Annabelle Terrence O'Dell does no' give her man his lovin'."

With a chuckle of anticipation she began undoing buttons and buckles.

Longarm offered no objection whatsoever.

Chapter 21

"Ach, ye needn't drive me home, luv. 'Tis no walk at all from here. Why, I'm already part o' the way thanks t' you." Anna would have gotten down from the buggy and started up the steep road afoot, but Longarm took her by the elbow, drew her to him, and stopped her with a kiss.

Anna sighed. "'Tis a gennelman you be, Custis Long. Which is only *one* o' the raisons I be so daft about ye." She giggled and touched his crotch, apparently completely unconcerned that anyone might be watching in the evening twilight.

Not that her touch aroused him now. Not after an entire day of passion in that beautiful little valley. Longarm was feeling completely spent by now. Hollow and drained. But certainly not unwilling to consider another encounter after sufficient time for recuperation. Say, in another two or three hours.

Longarm laughed and said, "I wouldn't think of letting you walk all the way up that mountain, Anna. Apart from the fact that the road is long and steep, ma'am, if you're half as sore as I am right now, you won't want to be doing any hiking. We'll let the horse do the work."

"Well . . . I *am* sore." She giggled. "Not that I'm complainin', mind."

She sat back in the buggy seat and leaned against him with her eyes closed and her hand once again resting familiarly on his leg while he guided the horse up the now-familiar road to the sanatorium.

Anna O'Dell was quite a girl, he thought as he drove. She was slight and appeared frail. But she was far from that. After today he had good reason to know her vitality.

And even after all of that she seemed to think it quite unremarkable that she should set out afoot to return to the hospital. Not that he would allow her to do such a thing, of course. But the girl damn sure was not a demanding type.

A slow smile spread across his face. Well . . . not demanding in *that* way, anyhow.

"Are you sure you don't want to have supper in town first?"

"I'll eat quick as I get back, luv. There's always som'at to nosh there."

Longarm was not entirely sure what Anna had just said, but he thought he had gotten the gist of it anyway. He kept the horse on an uphill course.

The animal spooked once near the place where the ambusher had been, but a quick tug on the driving lines brought it quickly back under control. The sudden jump forward when the horse boogered woke Anna, who was drowsing against Longarm's side.

"What—?" She was wide-eyed with fright.

"It's all right." He stroked her hair and soothed her. "He just smelled something, I think." He did not explain what it would have been he thought the horse smelled. Likely it was the carcass of the dead horse the ambusher had shot. Longarm wondered if the livery animal could recognize the odor of its stablemate, if that had any meaning to dumb creatures.

Then he smiled at his own foolishness. He had better things to do than fret about that.

The array of tents below the sanatorium was a fairy city of glowing gold as lamps inside the tents lighted the canvas from inside and turned the white cloth yellow with their flame.

"Pretty," he said.

"Aye." Anna raised her face to his, kissed him briefly, and then moved to the other side of the seat so there would be a properly decorous distance between them in case any of the patients was watching.

The horse pulled the last rise, and the hospital itself was in view. The ground floor was ablaze with lamplight as was

111

the uppermost, laboratory floor. Only the middle level, where the seriously ill were resting, showed few lamps at the windows.

"Will I see ye ag'in, Custis?"

"Count on it."

"Good."

Anna blew him a kiss good-bye and hopped out of the buggy before he could turn into the circle drive that would have delivered her to the front doors. She likely did not want to be seen in a man's company, he thought, and turned the buggy around before anyone inside might see him there.

He thought briefly about going in to see if there was any change in Major Tom Ferris's condition. But that might be an embarrassment to the girl. If there was any news, Bertram Henscher would have sent word. He would find out about it soon enough anyway. He decided to go on back down and turn the rig back in. It was already full dark now, and he would be keeping Albert away from his evening.

The iron tires on the buggy wheels crunched over the gravel, and the horse increased its pace on the way back down the mountain, as if the animal sensed that it was on its way back to the stable and was anxious for its supper. Longarm let it step along at a smart trot. He was anxious enough for his supper too.

The rig reached the switchback where the ambusher had been, and Longarm took a fresh grip on the reins.

A horse is not particularly intelligent, much to the annoyance of moony-eyed girls and silly women, but the creatures have a memory that would put any elephant to shame.

Nearly any jug-headed cayuse can retrace any trail it has ever followed, in any conditions of weather or fatigue. And if a horse spooks at something no more threatening than a scampering rabbit, and does not take the same path again for a year, why, follow it a year later and in that same spot the fool critter will be looking for a rabbit to jump, and will be willing to booger all over again just at the mere idea that a rabbit *might* jump out and scare it a second time.

112

So Longarm was ready for the horse to bolt again at the same place where it had wakened Anna on the drive up.

He was ready, but even so, when the animal jumped, its motion jerked him back against the seat.

"Whoa. . . ."

Bright yellow flashed out of the darkness of the roadside, and a bullet sizzled past his face.

The livery horse threw itself into a panicked gallop, and Longarm flung himself sideways out of the seat.

He struck the gravel hard and rolled, pulling his Colt even before he skidded to a stop on the loose soil at the side of the roadbed.

"Damn!" a voice complained.

A lump of heavy shadow directly at the side of the road across from Longarm extended and became the figure of a man rising to his feet with a rifle or shotgun in his hands.

The man stood and triggered a shot into the back of the buggy seat as the empty rig careened wildly from side to side in the downhill plunge of the terrified horse.

The man had been blinded by his own muzzle flash, Longarm realized, and had not seen Longarm jump clear.

Another ambush in the same damn place?

Time enough to think about that later.

Longarm lined the barrel of his Colt against the night sky just beside the dark figure so he could get a look at his sights.

The man jacked a lever down and up again to seat a fresh cartridge, aimed at the buggy seat where he thought Longarm still was, and fired again.

That'll be the day, Longarm thought.

He shifted the muzzle of his Colt in line with the bulk of the dark shape and fired once.

The man grunted and dropped.

Longarm rolled to his right quickly, came to a stop, and eased further in that direction in case the man was still alive and heard him shift position.

Damn this anyhow!

What the fuck was a second ambusher doing here?

He lay still and listened, but the only sound in the young

113

night was that of a slight breeze soughing through the fir trees nearby.

There was silence for several long minutes, then a faint, moist gurgle and a staccato thump of boot heels against the ground.

Either the downed man was in his death throes or he was one hell of a possum player.

Longarm glanced behind him to make sure the mountainside at his back was dark with brush—it would not do to let himself be silhouetted against anything pale if anyone was still alive on the other side of this damned road—then came slowly to hands and knees.

Nothing moved. Even the breeze had died away now so that there was no sound.

The runaway horse and buggy were somewhere down the mountain far enough that Longarm could no longer hear them.

He eased forward, keeping low and ready.

But there was no need.

The man who had shot at him was dead.

He had no companions.

Longarm stood and cussed while he reloaded the Colt and shoved it back into his holster.

"Well, shit."

He found a dead fir branch and lit a cheroot for himself, then used the same match to touch off the dry needles. In the quick crackling flare of their light he could get a better look at the dead man.

Unlike Jack Humphrey, this one he recognized easily.

The man's name was Bartliss. Lewis Clark Bartliss. He was easily recognizable. Someone had carved his nose with a knife at some time in the past, so the left nostril was nearly missing, and there was a scar that extended from it across his cheek nearly to his ear.

L. C. Bartliss was on a poster too, and it was a Wanted poster that Billy Vail kept very much toward the top of the stack.

Bartliss was wanted for liquor law violations in the Indian territories. At least that was what the federal govern-

114

ment wanted the man for. He was also wanted in Kansas for the rape and murder of three school-aged girls. But that, of course, was not against federal law.

The pine-needle torch flared and quickly died, and Longarm dropped it and stamped it underfoot to make sure he would not start a brushfire.

L. C. Bartliss was not going to be doing any more raping or murdering. Or violating any more liquor laws either, for that matter.

Longarm felt of the side of the man's throat even though he was sure Bartliss was already dead. Then, cursing again, he stood and gave thought to kicking the dead man's body just to give himself some way to vent his anger.

It had just occurred to him that for a second time, damn it, he was afoot here on fucking Mount Herman and was going to have to walk all the way back to the livery.

He was not so agreeable toward that idea as Anna had been.

Dammit, anyway.

He took a deep breath, cussed L. C. Barliss and Jack Humphrey and whatever notion had brought them both here, and started walking down the damn mountain again.

Chapter 22

The hostler had already sent for Deputy Wisman before Longarm ever reached Monument. The livery rig had come back empty, one wheel shattered by a blow somewhere on the wild run down the mountain, and the hub loose on the axle so that what was left of the wheel and tire were wobbling drunkenly.

Albert James said nothing about the damage when Longarm limped in out of the night, though, just, "You all right, Marshal?"

Longarm nodded.

"Buddy and me was just talking about should we get a search party t'gether tonight or wait for daybreak."

"No search needed," Longarm said, "but there's another body to be carted down. From the same damn spot, even."

That information aroused Wisman's interest immediately, and the young man's notepad came out of his pocket.

Longarm filled Wisman in on what had happened while a big-eyed Albert James listened.

"Are you as used t' this kinda thing as you sound, Marshal?" James asked at one point.

"Not hardly. Getting shot at from ambush ain't exactly my idea of what a sane man wants to do for a living."

"You said there's notices out on Bartliss?" Wisman asked, returning to his notepad.

"That's right." Longarm outlined what he could remember of the wants on the Kansas outlaw.

"I can't hardly believe this," Buddy said. "I mean, this is a peaceful community, Longarm. We just don't have this kind of trouble here. A little petty thievery now and then. A drunk or two. That's just about all I have to handle. That and husbands beating up on their wives of a Saturday night. You know what I mean. Now this . . ." He shook his head. "I just don't understand it."

"I don't either," Longarm admitted.

"You figure the fella tonight was a good friend o' the first man you shot an' come gunnin' for you after you grassed his pard?" the hostler suggested.

"Damned if I know," Longarm said. "I suppose that's as likely an explanation as any other. Although how one fugitive from Wyoming would get all that close to another one from Kansas and the I.T., well, you figure that one out. Bartliss and Humphrey didn't exactly stomp the same territory."

"Men on the run. They might bunch together," Wisman said.

"Anything is possible. Sure is strange, though."

"I'll make a report like before, of course," Buddy said. "And a copy to your boss." He smiled. "I haven't had time t' file his address away yet, so it's still handy."

"I'd appreciate it," Longarm said. He would have to follow the local deputy's report with one of his own, of course. When he did, Billy Vail was likely to ask some questions to which Custis Long had no real answers. This one was a puzzler. Two ambushes. Both by wanted men. But no known connection between them *or* why either of them should have a hard-on for Longarm.

And one thing Longarm definitely did not believe in was coincidence.

He sighed. There probably were no answers. Or none he would ever know, anyway.

Bartliss and Humphrey were dead and far beyond questioning. And it is hardly a secret that outlaws do not get along handily with the people who want to put them behind bars.

In a world where one drunk is apt to murder another for the price of a drink, it is just as reasonable to kill for the sake of freedom.

"I'll make sure the marshal is expecting your bill for

damages to the buggy," Longarm told the hostler after Buddy Wisman left.

"Aw, it looks worse'n it is. Replace those cracked spokes an' reset that tire, the wheel'll be all right again. I won't bother 'em for that." The old man smiled. "Least this time the horse come home alive."

"That's an improvement, I suppose."

"An' so did you," Albert said.

"There is that."

"Go on back t' the hoe-tel and get you some sleep," Albert suggested.

"You don't need me to go along and help bring the body down?"

"Naw. No need. I'll take keer of it. Don't worry yourself."

"Thanks, Albert."

"Any time, Longarm." He chuckled. "Or mebe I shouldn't say that. I'd ruther there wasn't no next time."

"So would I."

Longarm appreciated the old man taking care of the chore for him. The day had been a long enough one with Anna O'Dell's energies, and the walk back down the mountain had drained him even further. What Longarm needed now was a meal, a stiff drink, and a good night's sleep.

He figured to take care of all those things right about now.

"Good night, Albert."

"G'night, Marshal."

Longarm slept like he was the one who was dead and not L. C. Bartliss, but he woke refreshed and feeling whole again in the morning.

He had a huge breakfast at the café and walked over to the depot to see if the telegrapher was on duty yet.

If this kept up, Longarm mused as he walked, he was going to have to put in on his expense account for the price of having his boots resoled. He was likely wearing out boot leather at a fearsome rate.

The telegraph operator was behind his desk, and Longarm got a short wire off to Billy. Buddy Wisman's official report would fill the rest of it in when it arrived.

That task done, he continued on to the livery and got another horse from Albert.

"Try an' ride this one back, would ya?" Albert said with a smile.

"Hell, I tried the other times too."

"Yeah, well, be keerful, hear?"

"I will. Thanks." Longarm swung into the stock saddle. His own McClellan was at the hotel. But he was *not* going to plan on walking home a *third* time.

He took the bay out of town at a lope and headed up the now-familiar road to the Henscher Sanatorium.

Longarm was not much given to fits of nervousness, but even so he was riding with his boots barely in contact with the stirrups and his right hand ready to sweep for the Colt when he came up to the twice-used ambush site again. After all, no matter what anybody said, he had seen a good many old trees in the high country that had been hit by lightning a hell of a lot more often than the supposedly-impossible twice.

The bay horse never twitched an ear, though, and he rode by the spot without incident.

There was no indication that anything particularly interesting had ever happened there. Just a few scuff marks in the earth, and those might have been caused by anything.

Longarm shook his head and continued on to the hospital.

The tent patients who were receiving their treatment in the dry, pleasant mountain climate were busy this morning. Several of them were outside playing croquet on an expanse of clipped grass. Others had the sides of their tents rolled up. Longarm could see them inside, in easy chairs reading or facing each other across chess and checkers boards. A foursome of women patients was playing cards. The scene was tranquil. One might think death and gunfire could never come close to so idyllic a refuge as Bertram Henscher's sanatorium.

It was midmorning by now so Longarm was hoping to catch Bertram on his break from the laboratory work before he looked in on Major Tom Ferris.

In fact, the doctor and several of his staff were on the front porch when Longarm rode up the last grade and came in sight of the big hospital.

Bertram and two of his young men were facing Head Nurse Hopkins, the young blonde nurse Longarm had seen in the dining hall the other day, and a man in an expensive suit. The man would be a patient, Longarm guessed.

From the way the men and women of the group stood, the set of their shoulders, and the high-chin posture they adopted, Longarm guessed that he had ridden into the middle of an argument of some kind.

A patient complaint, likely. No one, not even a physician as dedicated to his work as Bertram Henscher so obviously was, could run any institution completely free of friction.

Hell, give some folks roast duck for dinner and they'd bitch because it wasn't squab. And the richer they are the bitchier, or at least it seemed that way at times. Judging from the suit the patient on the porch was wearing, this was one very rich patient Bertram was confronting at the moment. The tailoring alone on that outfit would feed most families for a year and a half, and the stickpin in the man's tie was sparkling in the sunlight so bright that Longarm could spot the thing from forty yards off. Up close a sparkler like that could blind a hawk.

Longarm drew rein well out of hearing—he did not want to intrude—and wasted time by fussing over a cheroot, going slow at trimming the end of the thing and getting it alight.

Nurse Hopkins saw him and said something to the others which was enough to break them apart, the patient and the women going inside, while one of the attendants hurried down the stairs to take Longarm's horse and Bertram and the other young man waited on the porch.

"I sure didn't mean to interrupt," Longarm said. "Sorry about that."

120

"No problem," Bertram assured him. "Just a family squabble." The doctor's welcoming smile was strained, though. Longarm thought the man looked drawn, like he hadn't been sleeping well lately. "What can I do for you, Longarm?"

"Just wanted to check in on the major. The way things've been going recently, Bertram, it sure would be nice if he was well enough that I could wrap him up an' carry him to Denver with me."

Longarm hadn't meant anything by that particularly, but Bertram Henscher acted like Longarm had just insulted him. The doctor stiffened and his face got red. "Don't start that shit with me now, Marshal. Not today."

"Bertram . . . I didn't mean . . ."

Henscher's shoulders slumped and he groped soundlessly for speech. After a moment he gave Longarm a wan smile. "I know. I'm just . . . irritable this morning. Got up on the wrong side of the bed, I guess. Will you forgive me?"

"Nothing to forgive, of course."

"Good." The smile seemed genuine this time. "Come inside, Longarm. We'll take a look at Major Ferris, and I'll give you a progress report on the man's condition."

Henscher led the way indoors with a confused but sympathetic Longarm following close behind.

Chapter 23

Head Nurse Hopkins pretended to ignore them when Henscher and Longarm passed her station, but she was surely pissed about something. Her shoulders drew in tight and her chin tucked down and she was gripping some papers in her hands so hard her knuckles went white.

Longarm thought at first she was still mad at Bertram over whatever that business on the porch had been. Then he realized that he had come inside with his cheroot clamped between his teeth, so the nurse could well be peeved with him but not wanting to say anything while he was with the doctor. Especially after she had just disagreed with Bertram about something else. Just in case that was it, he asked Henscher to wait a moment and went back to the door to chuck his cigar outside where it would not offend anyone.

If that was it, though, he thought about it too late. Nurse Hopkins didn't look any less pissed afterward.

There was the usual attendant at the foot of the staircase, and today another sitting in the second-story hallway. Henscher led the way to Major Ferris's room.

"Any change this morning, Tommy?"

"No, sir. No change."

Today there was no sign of Anna O'Dell in the major's room. Instead of by a nurse, the patient was being watched by one of the husky male attendants. The boy was not a pretender to great studies while he was on duty. He had a copy of the *Police Gazette* laid open in his lap.

"You can see for yourself, Longarm," Bertram said.

The doctor leaned over the inert form in the bed and laid

the back of his hand on Ferris's forehead to check for a temperature, then peeled an eyelid back.

"No change in dilation of the pupils," he said. "But I believe his breathing is easier than it has been. My guess is that he may yet come out of this and enter another period of remission. Not that there are any guarantees in medicine. Ours, unfortunately, is a most inexact science."

"You don't mind if I look at him myself, do you?"

"Of course not."

Henscher stepped out of the way and Longarm bent over Tom Ferris.

He did not believe that Bertram Henscher would try to deceive him.

But Tom Ferris damn sure might.

Once the man came out from under his heavy dosages of self-prescribed laudanum, he might very well have remembered the shootings in Trinidad and want to use the hospital as a second sort of refuge.

Longarm made a show of great concern as he leaned close over Henscher's patient and examined the man's slack, empty face. But while he was doing that he rested a hand on the bed at Ferris's side, and through the sheet that covered the man took a pinch of skin. He bore down on it between thumb and forefinger. Hard.

If the man was playing possum with him *that* would bring him out of it with a squawk.

It didn't. Thomas Ferris never moved. There was not so much as a flutter of his eyelids in reaction to the sudden, unexpected pain.

The man was quite genuinely in a deep coma.

"I sure was hoping . . ."

"There is still a good chance he will come out of it," Henscher assured him. "As I say, I believe I can detect an improvement in the respiratory function. The breathing. And that, of course, is the root of the problem with tubercle disorders. If that improves, the rest will quickly follow."

Henscher shook his head. "There is so *much* we don't yet understand, Longarm. So terribly much. But this disease is . . . I suppose you could say that it is notional. A patient in this state could die without ever again opening his eyes. Just . . . stop functioning. Or he could as easily take a notion to sit up right now and demand food. Ten minutes from now, Longarm, this man right here could be walking and laughing and feeling quite on top of the world. And I don't know *why*. In either extreme, Longarm, I haven't yet the faintest understanding of *why* it can work like this." Henscher shook his head again. "And that is only a small part of what I am trying to investigate here." He sighed. "So much work to do. So little true understanding. So little time to learn it all."

"I wish I could help you, Bertram. I truly do."

"So do I, my friend. So do I."

Henscher reminded the attendant that he was to be notified personally if there was any change in the major's condition, any change in either direction. Then he smiled. "Coffee?"

"Sure. Until something happens with your patient here I sure don't have anything better to do." Well, not at least with Anna on duty.

Longarm nodded a good-bye to the attendant and followed Bertram downstairs to the dining hall.

There were a few patients in the big room having a snack, and a good many more had gotten juice from the ever-present buffet and carried it out into the sunshine on the porch beyond the dining hall windows.

Some staff members too were taking a break, but today for some reason they were not all assembled at one table.

Three pretty nurses, Anna O'Dell not among them, sat at a table near the kitchen end of the hall while two of the boys in their crisp white shirts were drinking coffee at the opposite end of the long room.

Bertram and Longarm helped themselves to coffee and doughnuts, and Longarm followed the doctor to the far table where the attendants sat.

Nurses and attendants alike, Longarm thought, seemed quieter today. Not only not mixing together as they had before, they all seemed pensive. Before they had been so animated and relaxed. Now there was a faint air of tension in the hall.

Longarm did not want to inquire about it, of course, with the young men listening. Bertram Henscher was a good man. Longarm did not want to cause the man any embarrassment or discomfort in front of his employees.

They talked a little, Henscher reminiscing fondly about his school days and his family.

"Wonderful, wonderful people," he said. "They gave so much. So freely. My mother and grandfather both. Sacrificed everything for my education. My grandfather was an old man then. He should have retired and lived out his own dreams." He smiled at his memories. "My, how that man did love to fish. All he wanted was to be able to spend his time on the banks of a stream somewhere. I had it already worked out in my mind. When I graduated from school and became a success—everyone has dreams of great success, I suppose—I wanted to buy Granfers a bamboo fly rod, the very best available anywhere, and buy him a cabin on the Wabash. But he continued working to keep me in school. He was still working twelve-hour days when he dropped dead of what we then called consumption. As most still do, of course.

"After that my mother took over. She went to work in a factory for my sake, seeing me through public school and on into college by her own efforts. And then the disease took her too, and I changed my major to medicine. And now this. Lord, how I've prayed for the success my family never lived to see. For their sakes so much more than my own." The man seemed overcome by the power of his emotions. He turned his head and coughed.

"I hope you reach your goals, Bertram."

"Thank you, Longarm."

Longarm finished his coffee and left, Bertram leaving the dining hall at the same time and walking heavily up the stairs toward his laboratory.

Actually, Longarm thought as he collected the horse and mounted, Bertram Henscher would already be considered a success by worldly standards. He had created here a monu-

125

ment dedicated to the fight against diseases. For the patients who came to these plush surroundings, but also for every human being anywhere who would ever be afflicted by the tubercle disorders.

Most people would consider that alone to be a success.

But not Bertram Henscher, obviously.

Henscher would not be satisfied until he had unlocked the secrets of the wasting disease known as consumption.

A damned good man, Longarm reflected as he rode back down the mountain.

There was no ambush laid for him anywhere along the road, and this time he was able to ride the livery horse the whole way back to the barn, by damn. Longarm considered that to be something of an achievement after the way things had been going around here lately.

Chapter 24

Longarm had a visitor when he returned to his hotel.

"What the hell are *you* doing here?" he demanded.

Marshal Billy Vail smiled and laid aside the newspaper he had been reading while he waited for Longarm to return. "Checking up on you, of course. I was sure you'd come strolling in with some pretty young thing on your arm. Then I'd have an excuse to fire your butt if I ever decide I want to."

"Seriously, Billy, what's up? Is something wrong?"

"No, nothing wrong at all. My missus has been wanting to come take the waters over at Palmer Lake. She brought it up again this morning, and this time I said I'd bring her. She's over there getting herself plastered in muddy goo or whatever the hell it is ladies do at those places."

"You haven't been to the office this morning?"

"Nope. Didn't even look in today. I sent a note to Henry and gave myself the day off. If you can believe it, Longarm, we hardly have any warrants sitting around unserved right now. Very slow."

Longarm frowned.

"What is it you find wrong with that?" the balding, pink-cheeked U.S. marshal wanted to know.

"Nothing. But if you haven't been to the offices today you likely don't know what happened here last night."

Vail's genial, day-off expression faded. "What?"

Longarm filled him in. "I got a wire off to you early today, and the local deputy said he'd file an official report like before. Since then I've been up to the hospital. No change in Ferris, but Bertram says he thinks there could be improvement soon."

"Bertram?"

"Dr. Henscher. Hell of a nice fella."

Vail grunted. "I remember the posters on Bartliss, of course. Bad actor, that one. I'm glad he's crossed off the list. But why would the man be gunning for you?"

"Damned if I'd know, boss. I would have recognized him, of course. The descriptions on him were good. But I certainly wasn't looking for him here. Never would have thought to. Wisman and friends are guessing that Bartliss was buddied up with Jack Humphrey and decided to lay for me after I shot his pal. I suppose that's as good an idea as any other. Fact is, of course, we may never know. All I'm really sure of is that Bartliss was waiting for me in the same place where Humphrey had been. He just wasn't quite good enough to get the job done."

Billy Vail grunted again. "Well, I'm glad he wasn't. Whatever was behind it, I suppose it's over and done with now."

"Uh-huh."

Vail hemmed and hawed a little.

"Spit it out, Billy. What's on your mind now?"

"The truth is, places like that Palmer Lake resort drive me batty. Not my cup of tea at all. What do you say I buy you a drink, and we'll call the afternoon line-of-duty."

Longarm laughed and joined his boss for lunch and a serious session with a bottle of excellent Maryland rye.

"Shouldn't you be going to collect your lady?" Longarm suggested late in the afternoon. "The last excursion train leaves in a couple of hours."

"She'll join me at the depot. I, uh, hinted I might have to work today. I'll tell you what I should do, though. Better check at the telegraph office. I left word with Henry that he could find me here if anything came up today."

Longarm nodded and led the way to the depot. There was no traffic for Marshal Vail, but there was a lengthy message waiting for Deputy Long.

Longarm read it through.

"I'll be damned," he said.

128

"What's that?"

"It's from Henry. He got the wire I sent to you, of course and I guess he didn't have much to do today either. So he's been doing some research. According to this, Jack Humphrey was known to be operating fast and loose in Wyoming Territory until a month and a half ago. Then he was one of three men involved in a big score there. Payroll theft not involving federal jurisdiction. The other two were caught, but Humphrey disappeared and so did all the money they'd stolen."

"Bartliss . . . ?"

"Couldn't have been involved," Longarm said, anticipating Billy Vail's train of thought, "because about that same time he was seen down in Seminole country. Henry says there's nothing official on this, for obvious reasons, but Bartliss is thought to've been a lone holdup artist who knocked over an illegal whiskey peddler and made off with an unknown but probably very large amount of money. The whiskey peddler was found dead. White man, though, and no proof that he was selling whiskey, so again the jurisdiction is questionable."

"That's why we wouldn't have heard about it, I suppose."

"Probably being handled by the tribal police if anybody. A dead salesman for Taos Lightning wouldn't cause much excitement. Anyway, Bartliss hasn't been seen since. He just dropped out of sight completely. The same as Humphrey and at more or less the same time."

"But hundreds of miles apart," Vail said, "and certainly no indication that the two would have known each other."

"They weren't working together, that's for sure. In fact, I'd have to say that they were pretty different. Humphrey was basically a robber, and if I remember correctly, liked to work with others. Not a member of any gang, exactly, but he liked backup when he was pulling a job. There were murder wants on him, and I know from my own experience that he'd pull a trigger, but everything I ever heard about him says that he was a robber first and a shooter only if there wasn't a convenient way out. He didn't do it for fun.

"Bartliss, on the other hand, was a loner. And one mean son of a bitch. He liked to shoot, and he liked to terrorize women. Like I say, one mean son of a bitch."

"I don't recall as much about him as you seem to," Billy said, "but I don't recollect ever hearing about him working with anybody else."

"Correct me if I'm wrong, boss, but somehow those two just don't fit together very good."

"Riding the owlhoot can make for strange friendships," Billy reminded.

"Sure. But by necessity, not choice. These boys have been out of sight for better than a month, each of them. And the shootings done here weren't necessity. I wasn't looking for either of those boys."

"They might not've known that."

Longarm frowned. "I don't know, Billy. It just doesn't shake out to be so pat. I don't like the feel of it." He sighed. "But I don't know what else to add to this puzzle so it'd fit together, either."

"If you come up with any ideas, I'd be pleased to hear them."

"No more pleased than I'd be," Longarm assured him.

A string of large coaches appeared from the direction of Palmer Lake, and Billy Vail straightened his tie. "Looks like I have to pay attention to being a husband again, Longarm. I'll put some thought to this, though. If I think of anything that sounds halfway sensible I'll get back with you. And I'll lay it out for Henry first thing tomorrow, too. Sometimes a fresh eye on a situation can spot something everybody else missed."

Longarm waited with Vail until the coaches arrived, greeted Mrs. Vail, and then said his good-byes to both of them.

It was only later, walking back to the hotel, that he realized he and Billy both were talking like the problem of the unexplained ambushes was *not* as over and done with as both of them claimed it to be.

Chapter 25

Longarm found a leather-bound volume of Dickens, only slightly used and at a price too good to pass up. After supper he carried it up to his hotel room and laid it aside. Before he settled in for the evening there were a few things he needed to do. And tomorrow, with any luck, Major Ferris would show that hoped-for improvement and he could get this business wrapped up and take the train home to Denver.

He removed his tweed coat and draped it on the hook screwed into the back of the door, helped himself to a swallow of smooth rye whiskey from the bottle he carried in his bag, and lit a cheroot. The formalities observed, he palmed his Colt and shucked the fat, stubby cartridges into his palm and laid them aside.

A flat tin that had once held medicated throat lozenges now disgorged an oil-soaked bit of rag. He used that and a short section of cleaning rod to give the Colt a once-over.

Footsteps passed his door in the hallway and then returned toward the stairs. Nobody home in whichever room they had visited. There was no one in Monument who would be looking for Custis Long tonight.

Longarm had no more than had the thought when he heard the approach of a lighter tread and a soft tapping on his door.

"Custis?"

He smiled. The voice was familiar. Anna.

This was one time he did not at all mind being wrong.

He laid the empty Colt aside and opened the door for her.

"Ah, I was hopin' you'd be in, I was." She smiled and

131

slipped inside. Longarm closed the door and bolted it behind her. "You've no other plans, luv?"

"Only an evening with Mr. Dickens. He can wait."

Anna looked disappointed. "You've an engagement?"

Longarm chuckled and explained that Charles Dickens was an English author of some repute. It was only his book that Longarm had plans for.

"Ach. One o' them Sassenach bastards. That'un *can* wait." Anna smiled and began to peel off her dress. Like many Irish and Scots, the girl was definitely not friendly toward the English.

Longarm went back to the small rickety table and reloaded the Colt, returning it to its holster and removing his gun belt to drape it over the bedpost.

"And is that ugly thing more interestin' than I am, luv?" Anna protested.

He smiled. "Not hardly."

That was certainly true. The girl was naked now. In the light of the lamp she was pale and beautiful, her skin flawless, the glow of the light making the red of her unpinned hair gleam and shimmer with every slight movement.

She raised her arms in a deliberately provocative motion that showed already-pert breasts to fullest advantage and posed before him, turning and posturing and fully enjoying the reaction she could see behind his fly. The front of his trousers bulged, and Anna wet her lips with the delicately pink tip of her tongue while she peered at the spot.

"It's a lovely laddie you are, dear."

Longarm started to unbutton his vest but she stopped him, moving close to kiss him and grind the flaming red vee of her pubic hair against his cloth-captured erection.

"Let me," she whispered.

"Mmm." Longarm tried to return her kiss, but with a giggle Anna ducked under his embrace and dropped to her knees, naked before him.

She opened her mouth and applied it to the hard corduroy that contained him.

She exhaled slowly, and he could feel the heat of her breath seep through the cloth to envelop and surround him.

132

The sensation was exquisite, and he shivered, drawing a delighted response from playful Anna.

"Ach, yes," she said. "That's right . . ."

Longarm froze in place, his erection gone, as the hotel room door eased silently open.

He had just bolted that door shut moments before.

The damn thing was unlocked now.

Longarm blanched as the only possibly explanation hit him.

Anna unlocked the door when his back was turned and he was reloading the Colt.

The red-haired little Irish bitch had sold him out.

Two men stepped inside the room before he could reach for the Colt hung on the bedpost.

Anna now had her arms wrapped tightly around his knees, the little bitch. He couldn't have moved without falling.

The unwelcome visitors had revolvers in their hands. Small, concealable, nickel-plated Smith & Wessons.

They were big bastards, both of them, and looked more like head knockers than gunmen. Back-alley brawlers. Longarm had never seen either of them before, nor did he think either of these two was on any Wanted poster he had ever been shown.

In spite of that, he did not really believe that their intention here was social in nature.

"My oh my," Longarm said dryly. "Guests." He looked down at Anna, but the girl would not meet his eyes. "You should have told me we were having company, dear. I'd've sent for more glasses." He motioned toward the bureau where his bottle of rye sat. "Join me for a drink, gentlemen?"

"Shut up," one of them snarled. "You. Snag his gun off'n that bedpost."

Anna nodded and pulled away from Longarm, her head still down so that she would not have to look him in the eyes.

Moments earlier her naked flesh had seemed inviting

133

and dear. Now the same pale skin appeared mottled and unpleasant.

Anna hurried to the bedpost and lifted the heavy gun belt off of it. She seemed uncertain what to do with the thing now that she had it.

"No, dammit, don't bring it to me. I don't want you taking it near him. They tell me he's a tricky bastard. Just stand right there with it. If he makes a grab for you, throw the thing as far as you can and get the hell outa the way."

Anna nodded mutely and chewed at her underlip.

"Well," Longarm said cheerfully. "To what do I owe this honor, gentlemen?"

"No honor. Just a job," one of them intoned.

"I see. One of those quick and permanent jobs, I assume, since you aren't worried about me seeing your faces."

The bullyboy shrugged.

"I hope you'll at least let me have a smoke before I go."

His cheroots were in the coat hanging on the door behind them. But the bastards wouldn't know that.

Longarm gave the two an easy smile and dipped two fingers into his vest pocket as if reaching for a match.

"Watch hi—"

The man never had time to finish the warning.

The little brass-framed hideout derringer came easily into Longarm's hand.

He thumbed back the hammer and dropped into a crouch as the nearer gunman wasted precious fractions of a second trying to aim the unfamiliar Smith & Wesson he was holding.

Longarm fired first and a .44-caliber slug smashed into the man's throat. The gunman's Smith fired harmlessly before he could bring it in line, discharged by a reflexive jerk on the trigger before he died.

The second man shouted and scrambled for the door, his own revolver forgotten in his hand.

Anna stood frozen in place, her mouth gaping and one hand reaching for her soft, naked belly, where all of a sudden a second navel seemed to have appeared.

The wild shot jerked off by the dying man, Longarm noted without particular interest at the moment.

Before Anna's knees dropped out from under her, Longarm grabbed his Colt from her hand and shoved the derringer back into his vest pocket.

He could hear boot heels thud on the hallway flooring as the second gunman tried to escape.

Longarm raced out the door after him.

Chapter 26

The head knocker had a good start on him. Longarm charged down the hall and took the stairs three at a time down to the ground floor and out into the street.

He caught a glimpse of the man running hard away from the lights of the saloons and the few stores that were still open.

He might have had a shot for one instant, but a woman stepping out of a shop moved between him and the gunman and he did not dare risk hitting her.

"Move," he shouted, thundering down the sidewalk toward her.

The fool woman froze in place instead, an indignant look coming over her as Longarm snarled a curse out of the side of his mouth as he had to veer wide to avoid trampling her.

The gunman disappeared around a street corner, and Longarm ran after him.

He careened around the corner. The gunman was forty, fifty yards ahead and running strong.

The son of a bitch was faster than he looked.

But then he damn sure had plenty to lose if he failed to win this particular race.

Proper by-the-book procedure would be for the peace officer to order the fleeing fugitive to halt.

Right!

That would sure do it.

Longarm stretched his legs and put on more speed.

This one was *not* going to get away.

They ran past darkened storefronts, and the gunman

flickered in and out of spills of light as the two men charged past the last of the lights.

Several times Longarm might have risked a shot at the man except that the Colt in his hand held only the one load of six cartridges. All his spare ammunition was still in his coat pocket, and the damned coat was still hanging on the hook back in the hotel. Once the Colt ran dry, Longarm was disarmed.

The gunman turned another corner and charged up a hill, Longarm gaining ground on him now as his longer legs and better physical condition began to tell on the chase.

"Shit!"

The man abruptly changed direction and darted into a shadowy walkway.

The door of the house it led to was being opened. A man was coming out onto the stoop, saying something to someone just inside, putting his hat on.

Longarm recognized the place as the local whorehouse. The Red Lantern? Something like that.

Indignant voices were raised as the fugitive burst past, giving the presumably satisfied customer a shove out of the way that sent the man sprawling off the stoop where his fall was broken by some low-growing ornament junipers.

Longarm rushed in behind the gunman, out of darkness into the sudden glare of bright lamps.

He was just in time to see the gunman's boot heels disappear around a turn onto the second-floor landing and to hear the thump of running feet on the bare wooden flooring above.

Longarm raced up the stairs behind the man, scarcely hearing the shout of protest from the madam he had just left standing open-mouthed in the foyer below.

A door slammed closed as Longarm gained the second story.

If the son of a bitch knew where he was going here, if there was a way out... across a roof... down a rain gutter...

Longarm ran to the end of the hall and threw a door

137

open, startling a sweating, red-faced couple out of their intimacy, the powder-caked whore shouting something about, "Wait your turn, dammit." The man had bright scarlet, angry-looking pimples on his skinny ass, Longarm noted before he slammed the door shut on them again.

Wrong damn door.

He tried the one across the hall.

Here a whore with henna-reddened hair that was not at all like Anna O'Dell's was already sitting up staring toward the wide-open window while her companion of the moment was huddled beneath a filthy sheet that he had drawn over his face.

Right door!

Longarm ran to the window.

The gunman was tiptoeing across the shingled slant of a porch roof, heading for a downspout or post at the far end of the thing.

"Far enough," Longarm told him, leaning out the window with his Colt leveled.

The plug-ugly jerked his head around, eyes wide with terror.

"Don't. . . ."

The abrupt motion caused the man to lose his balance.

His arms flailed, the little shiny Smith & Wesson spinning out of his hand and off into the night.

His feet went out from under him on the loose, slippery cedar shingles, and he screamed as he slid toward the edge of the roof.

The Smith landed somewhere below and discharged from the impact with a sharp, nasty crack.

The gunman screamed again, panic bringing his voice to a sharp pitch, and dropped off the roof.

"Dammit," Longarm muttered.

He shoved the Colt into his waistband and eased carefully out onto the slope of the roof, prepared to drop to the ground and resume the chase if he had to.

The gunman was lying on his back. He was moaning and twitching, his heels drumming on the ground.

The man did not look like he was going anywhere.

Moving very carefully, Longarm sat on the shingles and felt with his feet until he located the support post under the roof, then lowered himself over the edge, wrapped his legs around the post, and shinnied down it to the porch level.

The porch was on the side of the whorehouse and was lighted by the spill of lampglow from the parlor inside.

Blank, curious faces stared out through the window.

Longarm ignored the spectators and hurried to the gunman's side.

The son of a bitch was dead by the time he got there.

From so brief a fall?

Longarm rolled the body over.

Just behind his shoulder blades was a chunk of unsplit firewood someone must have dropped and left in the yard.

The man had landed on top of it, snapping his spine and sending him into his death throes.

Longarm cussed and bent over, resting his hands on his knees and reaching for breath.

He was winded after the hard run.

The indignant madam came rushing outside, demanding to know what the fuck was going on here because this was a decent house and she didn't allow any...

Longarm ignored the woman, took another deep breath, and started jogging back toward the hotel.

Anna had still been alive when he left the room.

Maybe she could give him some answers.

The madam shouted for him to stop.

But that command didn't work any better for whores than it did for peace officers.

He ran on into the night.

Chapter 27

There was a crowd in the hotel room when Longarm got there. The hotel clerk was kneeling beside the naked girl, and a number of other men, hotel guests probably, were crowded inside the small room as well.

Anna's breathing was shallow and labored.

There was little external sign of the damage that had taken place inside her.

The small-caliber bullet had made a moist red dimple low on the swell of her belly, but except for that there really was nothing to see. There was no blood except for that small patch of wetness in the new-made belly button.

"Marshal. Did you——?"

"Have you sent for a doctor?" Longarm interrupted.

"Don't have one in town. Just up at the sanatorium. I've sent a man up there and another fella over to Palmer Lake in case there's a doctor staying at the resort there. But I don't think this girl's gonna make it long enough for anybody to get here anyhow. See for yourself what you think."

The clerk stepped aside, and Longarm knelt beside the motionless girl.

Anna's eyes were closed, and her breath was ragged.

She gasped and stiffened.

Her face and lips had lost all their color.

Longarm peeled her eyelid back. Her pupils were very large, and the eye unfocused.

"Anna?"

There was no response.

He lightly stroked her cheek.

The girl had sold him out to those two men. But she hadn't bargained on this.

"Look. Marshal. I know you're an officer an' all that, but . . . I mean . . . we try an' run a quiet place here."

Longarm ignored the hotel clerk. He heard a murmur of low voices from the men who had come into the room. One of them was saying something about Anna's pussy.

Longarm jerked the sheet off his bed and covered the dying girl's nakedness. The action brought a subdued mutter of protest from some of the spectators, but none of them was bold enough to speak up about it.

"If you people got nothing better to do," Longarm said, "you could haul that dead man outa here. No, wait a minute. I better look him over first."

Unlike the clean, tidy wound that was killing Anna O'Dell, the man's wound had been messy. There was a good bit of blood on the floor that would have to be cleaned up, too.

Longarm started to rise, but Anna stirred again, her eyelids fluttering and her pale lips drawing thin with pain.

She rocked her head angrily from side to side.

"Hunnerd dollars," she complained. "Not 'nuff. They said . . . hunnerd dollars. Oh, Jaisus. He'p me."

Her back arched, lifting off the floor in a grotesque parody of the happy, wanton way she had thrust her hips upward to meet him.

Her eyes snapped open, but this time her frantic stare was focused an impossible distance away and there was a dull glaze on the surface of her eyes.

Her teeth clacked together, the sound of it loud in the sudden stillness of the room.

When she went limp, her hips dropping back onto the flooring, it was for the last time.

Her last breath escaped still lips soundlessly. There would not be another.

"Oh, hell."

Longarm laid a hand gently onto the dead girl's face and drew her sightless eyes closed, then pulled the sheet the rest of the way up to cover her.

"Guess I can tell the doctor not to bother coming, huh?"

Longarm nodded and stood.

He moved to the body of the man who had tried to kill him.

There was nothing in the man's pockets to indicate who he might have been or who might have sent him here on this mission.

The fellow had a folding Barlow knife, a long unwashed handkerchief, some lint and one hundred dollars in gleaming double-eagle coins in his pockets. Nothing else.

Nothing at all to say who he was or where he came from.

"Have you sent for Deputy Wisman?" Longarm asked.

"I never thought o' that," the clerk told him.

"Do it, please." Longarm started for the door.

"Where are you gonna be?"

Longarm paused. "There's another body over at the whorehouse. I better take a look at him too before he's moved."

"Jesus," someone in the crowd blurted. "You play hell once you get started, don't you."

Longarm started back for the Red Lantern. More slowly than the last trip had been.

He had scant hope that he would find anything useful on the other dead man, but he had to make the effort.

He was feeling tired all of a sudden, but it had nothing to do with the running and the chasing.

He was feeling weary of death.

Anna O'Dell had turned on him. Sold him out to be killed for a hundred dollars in gold coin.

Yet the pretty Irish girl had shared more than just that with him.

Her death affected him more deeply than he would have expected—or wanted—under the circumstances.

And he still did not know what any of this was all about.

Chapter 28

Longarm learned no more from the dead man at the whorehouse than he had from the others. Other than a few articles of no interest, the man had a hundred and twelve dollars on him, a hundred in the gold double-eagles like the first one had had, and twelve in silver. Neither of the hired killers had been exactly rich.

The indignant madam wanted to give Longarm hell, but she had a sudden change of attitude when he flashed his badge. After that she was all eagerness to help. Indicating, he suspected, that whoring was not legal in this neighborhood, though it was obviously tolerated as long as there was no trouble at the house.

"Have this guy taken off to . . . hell, wherever you take bodies around here," Longarm told her.

"Right away, Marshal."

She motioned for her bouncers to take care of it and disappeared quickly.

Longarm went back to the hotel. There was no point in trying to get a wire off to Billy Vail tonight. The telegraph operator was long since off duty.

Both bodies had been removed from his room. A swamper was there when Longarm went in. The man was mopping the floor but not doing much of a job of it. More rearranging the blood than removing it.

"Careful," the man said.

Longarm stepped over the wet stain on the flooring and sat on the edge of the bed. The swamper finished and left. A moment later the door opened again. Longarm assumed it was the swamper coming back for something. Instead Bertram Henscher came into the room. Apparently the

143

hotel clerk had forgotten to send word that a doctor was no longer needed her.

"Longarm. You're all right."

"Sure. Didn't they tell you?"

"They said there had been a shooting and that I was needed here." Henscher was carrying a black leather case and looked like a typical small-town doctor instead of a medical researcher.

Henscher stepped inside, and another man trailed behind him.

Longarm was tired, and it took him a moment to remember where he had seen this second man before. It was the snappily dressed man who had been on the porch arguing with Henscher and Nurse Hopkins that morning.

"Who're you?" Longarm asked.

Bertram started to answer, but the visitor interrupted. "Donahue is the name," he said quickly. "Jonathan Donahue. I'm a dealer in pharmacological supplies. I thought I might do something to help. Hope you don't mind."

Longarm shook his head. Frankly he was too tired to give a crap if all of Monument wanted to parade through his hotel room.

"What happened, Longarm?" Bertram asked softly.

Longarm filled him in.

The doctor looked bleak when he heard about his nurse and irate about the two men who had tried to kill Longarm.

"You can't be serious," he said.

"Sorry, but I expect I am. The girl's dead, Bertram."

"Who were—" Donahue began, but Henscher gave the salesman a dirty look. "Sorry," he apologized quickly. "I shouldn't intrude. Didn't know the girl myself, of course. Great pity though." He coughed delicately into his fist and backed out of the room.

"Is there anything I can do, Longarm?"

He shook his head. "Nothing, Bertram. Thanks for coming, though. I just wish...things had been different when you got here."

"Longarm," Henscher said impulsively, "I really think

there has been a great improvement in Major Ferris's condition since this morning. . . ."

"He's awake?"

"No. Not that much improved. But definitely better. I am sure he is *much* better now. It won't be but a matter of time before he comes around. And . . . I think it would be safe for you to move him now. There are excellent hospital facilities in Denver. Why don't you take him there to complete his recovery?"

"I thought you said moving him could kill him."

"I did. Of course I did. But that was before. He's much improved now. I'm sure it would be safe for you to move him. In fact, I would appreciate it if you did. The man is a charity case for us, after all. He isn't able to pay, certainly not in his present condition. It would be a favor to me if you were to take him into federal custody and move him now. Get him off my work load, so to speak."

Longarm rubbed his face. It was not all that late, really, but he felt drained by all that had happened this evening. His eyes felt gritty. He wanted a bath and a long sleep.

"I suppose I could do that," he said.

"I understand the new ambulance has arrived at the livery," Henscher pressed. "You could hire it to transport the patient."

"Sure." Longarm yawned. "Thanks."

Henscher gave Longarm a troubled look. "Will you be all right tonight? I mean . . ." He looked embarrassed now.

"I'm fine," Longarm assured him. He smiled. "I never get so tired that I sleep *that* soundly. Anybody comes in here in the night, he'd best make sure I'm awake and wanting him to come in." He patted the butt of the Colt at his waist.

"Yes. All right. You . . . take care of yourself. All right?"

"I'm fine, Bertram. Honestly. And thanks for coming all this way so late."

"Of course. Any time." Henscher backed awkwardly toward the door, lingering as if there was something more he wanted to say but did not know how to get into it.

Whatever it was, if anything, went unspoken. Henscher stood there for a moment, then nodded and let himself out.

Longarm sat on the edge of the bed a few seconds longer, unwilling to expend the effort needed to rise. Then he stood, stepped around the wet bloody spot that the swamper had done such a poor job of cleaning, and bolted the door closed.

This time there was no one else in the room to slide the bolt open again when Longarm was not looking.

He checked to make sure the window was securely closed. He much preferred fresh air when he slept. But not so much so that he would invite the visit of a killer just so he could be cooler at night.

Then he stripped off his clothes and went to bed. His bath could wait until morning, he decided. He simply hadn't the energy to go take one now.

The sheet he had put over Anna's corpse had not been replaced, and the blanket that covered him was scratchy.

Worse, he was sure the bedding smelled of Anna's warm, lusty scent.

But that was probably only his own imagination. It had been days since she shared this bed with him. Only hours or less since the girl died while he stood by unable to do anything to prevent it.

He closed his eyes in exhaustion, but even so it was quite some time before he was able to slip away into the blessed relief of sleep.

Chapter 29

Longarm woke up worried. Something was nagging at him. Chewing its way slowly into his subconscious.

Whatever it was it was something too small, something buried too deep, for him to so much as identify it. Yet. But it was there. He was aware of it.

And whatever it was manifested itself in a sense of urgency.

He woke shortly before dawn with a desire to get things moving. And to do it *now*.

He dressed quickly, packed his gear, and carried it over to the livery where Albert James was already awake. He found the old hostler in the corral behind the barn forking hay to the stock.

James gave him a concerned look. "I heard you had you some more trouble last night. Anything I c'n do t' help, Longarm?"

"There sure is, Albert. I need to hire that ambulance of yours to bring a patient down from the hospital and carry him to Denver."

"Sure. But I want t' warn you. I haven't got the thing cleaned up yit. It's awful dusty from the hauling."

"That doesn't matter. Just so it's sound."

"That it is, son. She's a good'un." Albert spat. "I'll fit it up for you quick as I'm done here."

Longarm pitched in to help the friendly hostler finish his morning choring, then the two men opened the low shed where the livery's rolling stock was kept and wheeled the light ambulance out.

The rig still carried markings on it from a military hospital somewhere—Nebraska, had he said? or was it Montana? not that it mattered—and it was caked with dried mud as well as fresher dust from all the traveling it had done.

It was sturdy, though. Soundly built with wooden sides and a running gear tough enough to stand up under cross-country military campaigning.

Slings and racks in the enclosed wagon-bed were able to carry eight cramped litters, but for civilian use a pair of cots had been bolted in place. The cots were unsprung. A sick or badly wounded man riding in a rig like this would be kept alive, but there had been damned little done to provide for comfort.

"I'll pad this up for you," Albert said. "Got some old mattress ticking I can stuff with hay. Three, four of those oughta help some."

Longarm sorted out the harness while Albert arranged the inside of the rig to be as comfortable as possible. Then the old hostler brought out a rough-looking gelded cob and adjusted the harness to fit him.

"Don't be put off by the looks o' this old boy," Albert said. "He ain't anything for pretty, but he's tough as a whang and he's steady. Kid throws a firecracker under his feet he'll lay his ears back but he won't run off." The old fellow chuckled. "Come t' that, you *want* him to run off he *still* won't do it. Got two speeds to him. Slow or stopped altogether. I hope you ain't in a hurry with him."

"He'll do," Longarm said. It occurred to him, though, that if he wanted to outrun anyone he was going to be in a heap of trouble.

Hopefully it wouldn't come to that.

Longarm shook his head, angry with himself for this nagging, gnawing concern that he couldn't pin down. He had no idea what he was so worried about. Just that he was damn sure worried this morning.

A pang of hunger rumbled in his stomach, reminding him that he hadn't taken time for breakfast.

That could wait, though. He would grab a doughnut at the hospital while he was getting Tom Ferris loaded into the ambulance. The unidentified anxiety simply would not permit him to sit and eat right now. He wanted to *move*.

Albert made a last-second adjustment to the cheek piece on the driving bridle, and Longarm climbed onto the seat of the ambulance.

Longarm reached behind him to the front of the ambulance body where his bag and saddle were stowed and pulled his Winchester from its scabbard, sliding it under the driving seat where it would be handy if it were needed in a hurry.

Albert gave him a questioning look but said nothing, and Longarm shook the seal-brown gelding into motion toward the all-too-familiar drive up Mount Herman.

It was still early by the standards of most folks when Longarm reached the vicinity of the hospital grounds.

The side walls on most of the patient tents were still rolled down against the chill of the night air, and several pretty nurses were busy wheeling breakfast carts from tent to tent. Bertram Henscher's patients damn sure got the royal treatment when they were here, Longarm thought. There were near as many nurses in evidence as there were tents to hold the patients.

The brown horse continued up the last slope with the same slow but seemingly inexhaustible power that he had displayed since they left Monument, and Longarm came in sight of the big hospital itself.

The slanting sun of early morning, streaming in from above the rolling plains, caught the windows on the top floor of the huge building and reflected brightly off the glass, giving the place a look of being forbidding and coldly uncaring.

Which of course was ridiculous. Longarm doubted he had ever met anyone who cared more about his work than Bertram Henscher. The man was practically a candidate for sainthood.

He brought the ambulance to a halt in front of the steps. No one was out on the porch so early, but in less than a minute one of Bertram's husky young attendants hurried out to take charge of the rig.

"Good morning, Marshal."

"Good morning. Uh, Tim, isn't it?"

"Yes, sir."

"Is Bertram up yet?"

"I wouldn't know, Marshal. You can ask inside."

"Thanks." Longarm climbed the short set of stairs and went in.

Head Nurse Hopkins was at her station, looking crisp and freshly starched. The woman gave the impression that she could be found there behind her desk at any hour of the day or night. She had that pinched, snooty look about her that denied she might ever have any bodily functions. Longarm tried to imagine her squatting and straining over a thunder mug with her skirt around her waist, but he couldn't begin to visualize it.

"Good morning, Nurse."

She gave him a nod that was no more personal than she might have given to the brown horse Longarm had left outside.

"I'm looking for Bertram," he said.

"I'm sorry. The doctor is not available this morning."

"He's expecting me."

"I'm sorry, Marshal, but Dr. Henscher is *not* available this morning." Her nose hiked a fraction of an inch higher and she looked quite ready to argue the point if Longarm wanted. But not to yield on it by a bit.

Longarm grunted. He knew better than to get into fights he couldn't possibly win. "Did he leave any instructions about transporting Major Ferris?"

"He did not," Nurse Hopkins returned.

"Look. I know it's early. And Bertram isn't available. But he told me last night I could collect my prisoner this morning. I brought the ambulance he suggested I hire, and now I want to take the major and leave. Is that all right with you, Nurse Hopkins?"

She sniffed.

Longarm decided if the damned woman ever got caught in a hard rain she was doomed to drowning. Her nose was held so high it would surely funnel the rainwater right into her.

"I have no instructions about—"

"Then get Bertram down here," he said.

"The doctor is unavailable, and—"

"Look!" Longarm was losing patience with this woman. More to the point, now that he was here he wanted *gone* from here. Him and his prisoner, too.

Whatever it was that had been bothering him through the night and ever since he came awake this morning was working overtime now. The feeling of uneasiness was becoming more and more acute, and he wanted to get Tom Ferris loaded and be on his way right *now*.

"I . . . want . . . Thomas . . . Ferris . . . now," he said with slow, exaggerated enunciation.

Nurse Hopkins blinked.

"I told you already," he said, more calmly this time, "I talked to Bertram last night. It was *his* idea for me to bring the ambulance and fetch the major today."

"I have no authority to—"

"But I do," Longarm interrupted. He pulled out the warrant Billy had made out with Thomas Ferris's name on it and laid it on the counter between them.

Nurse Hopkins stared down at the paper.

"I am here to place Ferris under arrest on charges of murder," Longarm said. "That is not subject to debate, Nurse. Interference with my official duties would be a violation of federal law. And I doubt that either of us wants to get into that."

The woman sniffed again. But this time she nodded too. She pushed the warrant across the counter toward Longarm, and he refolded the thing and returned it to his pocket.

"Thank you." He started toward the stairs.

"Wait."

Longarm stopped. "Yes?"

"Visitors are not permitted beyond the ground floor. Even visitors with warrants to serve. You say you brought an ambulance?"

"That's right."

"I shall have your prisoner brought down and placed in the ambulance, Marshal. You can wait in the dining hall while I make the arrangements, if you like."

"Thank you, Nurse Hopkins."

The woman sniffed again but left her station to scurry toward the stairs where today a nurse was on duty—with a textbook laid open in her lap—instead of the usual male attendant. Longarm was pleased enough, though, to be sent to the dining hall. He was definitely hungry now in spite of the nagging concerns he was still experiencing.

Why *was* he so damned uneasy this morning? There was no logical reason for it. None at all. Yet the gut-level feeling—a hunch or notion or whatever one might wish to call it—just would not go away.

Chapter 30

The dining hall was busy at this hour. A serving line had been opened into the kitchen area, feeding through one door beside the usual buffet spread and out another door on the other side of the coffee table.

Patients were scattered throughout the big hall, sitting alone or sometimes paired, but rarely filling a table. There were no nurses in evidence. Probably they were all busy with their morning duties, Longarm thought. But there were a good many of the male attendants crowded around a string of the small tables that had been pulled together to form one long one. The young rugby players were quiet. Longarm got the impression that they were feeling about as gloomy this morning as he did.

The usual array of pastries had not been laid out yet, and Longarm resigned himself to having to make do with just coffee and juice. He was reaching for a cup when he saw out of the corner of his eye that someone was approaching.

"Marshal."

"Mr. Donahue."

"I just saw Miss Hopkins in the hallway, Marshal. She asked me to deliver a message."

"Yes?"

"She said it will take a little while to make your prisoner ready for travel, and suggested that you help yourself to breakfast if you haven't eaten already." Donahue smiled and motioned toward the serving line.

"That'd be nice, thanks. Say, you said you saw Nurse Hopkins. You haven't run into Bertram this morning, have you? I wanted to see him before I go."

"Sorry. I'm told he isn't available this morning to me either." The smile returned. "Perhaps he is working on that breakthrough he's been looking for. I am told he sometimes gets flashes of inspiration during the night and disappears into his laboratory, sometimes for days when the ideas are flowing. And the instructions about disturbing him are very strict."

"I see. Well, thanks anyway."

Longarm headed toward the kitchen and got into line behind a wheezing fat man with hugely bushy Burnside whiskers who was heaping his plate with sausages and scrambled eggs. The man was intent on selecting just the right links of sausage and just the right freshly baked muffins from the buffet. Longarm leaned against the doorjamb, content to wait while the fat man made his choices.

Donahue started toward the long table where all the attendants were seated, but before he got there the blonde nurse Longarm had seen several times before came into the far end of the hall, looked around until she spotted the medical supplies salesman, and hurried to him. She took his elbow and went onto tiptoes to whisper something into the peddler's ear. Her expression was one of urgency and importance in whatever she was saying.

Longarm idly wondered what could be so important. Unless Donahue carried a stock of supplies with him when he traveled—and that would be a rare thing indeed—anything ordered would require a great deal of time to be shipped from wherever it was that pharmaceuticals were manufactured.

Still, there was a hell of a lot that Longarm did not know about hospitals and medicines and laboratories and such. And these people certainly seemed to know what they were doing.

The fat man finished with his choices, having to use a second plate to hold it all, and waddled away. Longarm moved in where the glutton had just been and quickly loaded a more modest breakfast onto a plate.

Nurse Hopkins might be a stubborn broad, but he had to give her credit for her efficiency.

When they came and told Longarm that the ambulance was ready, Major Tom Ferris was tucked in place on one of the built-in cots on soft layers of blankets.

They had used Albert's makeshift hay mattresses but covered them deep with additional layers of clean blankets, then made the whole thing up with fresh sheets and more blankets until Ferris was as padded and secure as anyone could be.

Canvas straps had been run over the patient—prisoner now—and beneath the cot to prevent him from being bounced out of the bed. He was secured at the chest, waist and knees, and the whole ambulance would have to come apart before the patient could come adrift.

Some personal articles had been stored forward near Longarm's gear. He noticed a set of saddlebags, a gun belt, and a Spencer carbine that he assumed would be Ferris's. Ferris was still wearing hospital pajamas, but a decently tailored and freshly cleaned suit were on a hanger secured to a roof bow at the front of the rig.

Half a dozen of the burly young attendants were standing by the ambulance when Longarm came out. These boys too seemed downcast and uneasy in marked contrast to the cheerful, easygoing natures they had always displayed before when Longarm was here.

Nurse Hopkins was waiting for him at the back of the ambulance. She was holding a black leather medical bag similar to the one Bertram carried.

"It looks like everything is fine, thanks," Longarm said after checking inside the rig. He started to close the door, but Nurse Hopkins stopped him.

"Do you want me to sign a receipt for my prisoner?" Longarm asked.

"I do not," she snapped. "You could act like a gentleman, though, and help me inside."

"Inside? Why would you want—?"

"I intend to travel with you," she said in that no-nonsense voice that was every bit as crisp as her uniform. She started into the back of the ambulance.

"Whoa. I never said anything about . . ."

"Really, Marshal." Her inflection had the same tone as a schoolteacher speaking to a particularly dull child. *"We* are responsible for the well-being of this man regardless of what *you* wish to think. The doctor is *most* solicitous of all our patients. I intend to accompany you until this patient is lodged in a hospital of your choice. Why, he couldn't possibly be expected to remain back here by himself. You will be busy driving. You won't be able to watch him. I shall. And I intend to do so." Her expression was as set and stubborn as if it had been carved from granite. There surely was no give in this woman.

"Yes, ma'am," Longarm meekly said. He helped Nurse Hopkins into the back of the ambulance and waited until she was settled prim and rigid on the empty cot facing Ferris before he closed and latched the door.

The young attendants looked gloomy, and for a moment Longarm thought one of them was going to step forward and say something, but he did not.

Longarm went around to the front of the rig and climbed onto the driving box.

No one waved as he drove away, but the attendants stood staring after him.

Chapter 31

Bertram Henscher knew a hell of a lot more about medicine than Custis Long ever would, of course, but Longarm's amateur opinion was that Tom Ferris didn't look a lick better to him today than he did the first time Longarm ever saw the man. And then Bertram had said that moving Ferris would likely kill him. Still, Bertram's judgment was the one that counted here.

Longarm looked back frequently to check on his prisoner-patient Ferris.

There was a wide pass-through between the driving seat and the ambulance box, large enough for a man to duck through if he wanted, and probably put there so doctors or orderlies could move back and forth between the seat and the patients while a column was on the march. A canvas curtain was rolled and tied at the top of the pass-through so rain or snow could be kept off the patients, but today was fair and it was always a part of the treatment of consumptives that they be given as much fresh air as possible. Longarm had no particular desire to visit with Nurse Hopkins while they traveled, but he certainly wanted to do nothing that would harm Ferris.

Formality or not, he had to keep on thinking the man innocent—and protect his interests just like he would those of any other innocent man—until a court of law proved him guilty. Just because a saloon crammed full of witnesses swore that Tom Ferris had gunned down those two soldiers, the law said that its deputy had no right to call Ferris guilty.

Longarm thought there was some small irony in the fact that this was a military ambulance—even if a surplus one sold off by the government—that Ferris was being hauled away in toward trial for the murder of two soldiers.

He rolled down the mountain to Monument and paused there to light a cheroot while he considered just what he should do next.

A train could carry them to Denver easier than Longarm could drive the distance. But he had already missed the morning northbound. There would not be another until evening. Besides, getting an unconscious Ferris on the train and making him comfortable there would be a slow, involved process that was sure to annoy hell out of the conductor. By the time the evening northbound was due to depart, Longarm could have Ferris already settled into a Denver hospital and under a doctor's care again. The drive was not all that long a one, and the brown gelding was a tireless puller.

Longarm flicked his spent match into the dirt and drove across the railroad tracks toward the road north.

Nurse Hopkins stuck her head through the pass-through. "Why aren't we stopping at the depot?" she demanded.

Longarm explained his reasoning on the subject, and the nurse's mouth pursed so there was a web of wrinkles around her thin, prissy lips.

"I assumed we would take the train. I can watch the patient in the baggage car while you ride in the coach, Marshal."

"Then you assumed wrong, ma'am. For one thing, you might be responsible for the patients, but *I'm* responsible for the prisoner. He won't leave my sight till he's in the jail ward at the hospital and receipted for by the city police there. For another thing, this's the way I intend to do it. Naturally, ma'am, you're welcome to get off here if you want. I can arrange for Mr. James to take you back up to the hospital if you like." He couldn't resist adding, "My pleasure if that's what you want." There was something about this woman that he just didn't care for.

Now that he thought about it, the damned female hadn't said a single word yet about Anna O'Dell being killed last night. Anna was one of the nurses under Head Nurse Hopkin's charge, yet the woman acted like she didn't care a thing that the girl had been shot to death.

That was damned odd now that he thought about it.

"Make up your mind, ma'am."

Nurse Hopkins's mouth pinched even tighter—Longarm hadn't thought that would be possible—but she said, "Proceed, Marshal."

"Yes, ma'am."

Longarm guided the gelding out of town onto the grade up Monument Hill where the Platts River and Arkansas River drainage basins divided.

The road was smooth as roads go, but even so there was plenty of jostling and bouncing going on. Ambulances are rugged but they are not carriage sprung. Longarm kept turning to see that Ferris was riding as comfortably as possible.

The man was still completely unconscious. All the movement and disturbance had not reached through the thick veil of disease, and once again Longarm found himself questioning Bertram Henscher's judgment.

The ambulance crested a small hill and began rolling down a long and particularly smooth grade. Longarm pulled a cheroot from his pocket and bit the tip off it, then reached for a match.

He wrapped the reins around the empty whip socket— the brown gelding was every bit as steady as Albert had said—and cupped his hands against the breeze to flick the match head aflame and apply it to the cheroot.

When he bent his head toward the flame he caught some movement out of the corner of his eye and felt a shift of weight in the ambulance behind him.

He turned in time to see Nurse Hopkins move from the cot where she had been sitting all this time and shift across to perch on the side of Ferris's cot.

The woman had the black bag open in her lap and was reaching into it.

Now, what the . . . ?

She glanced up, a nervous look on her face, and Longarm pretended to be concentrating on his cheroot.

Apparently satisfied, the nurse pulled a thick glass syringe from the bag. The thing had a wickedly long needle and was filled with a colorless fluid.

No one had said anything about medications being ordered. In fact, it was Longarm's clear understanding that there *were* no medications appropriate to the treatment of consumptives. That was one of the problems with the wasting disease and one of the things Bertram was searching for in his research. Hell, he thought he remembered Bertram saying something about that in one of their talks over coffee.

So why was . . .

Hopkins made no attempt to expose Tom Ferris's arm to receive the injection the way Longarm certainly would have expected.

She simply stabbed down with the needle, driving it through blankets and sheets alike into the upper part of Ferris's chest.

That wasn't fucking right at all.

"Hey!" Longarm roared.

His shout startled Hopkins into dropping the syringe. The thing wavered, then lost its grip on Tom Ferris's flesh and fell onto the bedding. The brown horse pinned its ears but remained steady in its motion.

Longarm threw himself backward through the pass-through, sprawling onto his back in the narrow aisle between the cots while Nurse Hopkins screamed and jumped toward the back of the ambulance.

Longarm twisted, rolling to hands and knees and trying to get to his feet in the close confines of the aisle.

Hopkins saw her chance and grabbed for the syringe.

She held the thing like a butcher knife in the hands of someone inexperienced with knife fighting, point down and arm upraised for a hammerlike striking blow.

"What the hell are you . . . ?"

Hopkins lunged forward, trying to drive the now-bent needle into Longarm's body.

He did not believe she was trying to make him feel

better with whatever medication was in that syringe.

"Quit, dammit."

He blocked her clumsy attempt to stab him and quickly stepped back.

Hopkins lost her balance, banged her knee on the side of Tom Ferris's cot, and fell to the floor while the ambulance rumbled over a series of washboard ruts across the road.

"What the hell has gotten into you?"

Longarm stepped forward and pulled the nurse upright, being careful as he did so that she did not have another chance to stab him.

The nurse's hands were empty, though.

She was staring down with horror, not reacting to him at all.

Hopkins let out a loud, plaintive cry and collapsed.

Longarm hauled her up onto the empty cot. And then he saw the source of the woman's terror.

The needle attached to the glass syringe was buried in Nurse Hopkins's left breast. And the plunger was pushed home, the colorless fluid emptied into the woman's body.

She must have stabbed herself with the thing when she fell.

And now whatever it was she had been trying to inject first into Tom Ferris and then into Longarm was now inside *her* body.

Longarm pulled the syringe free and laid it aside.

Hopkins was unconscious, although whether from fright or medication he was not sure. Her breathing was shallow now, though, and her color was swiftly deepening almost to a purple.

While Longarm watched, the woman convulsed and shuddered, her neck straining and arching back until her mouth gaped open and her tongue protruded from between yellowed teeth.

Lordy! Longarm thought.

He turned to check on Ferris, but the man seemed unharmed. If anything, in fact, he looked better now than he had before. There seemed to be a little more color in his face than there had been, and his breathing was stronger.

Even as Longarm watched, Ferris's eyelids fluttered. He seemed to be coming out of his coma while on the other cot Nurse Hopkins was dying.

Lordy! Longarm thought again.

The side of the ambulance tilted as the right front wheel rolled over a sizable rock, and the rig came down with a jolt nearly hard enough to throw Longarm off his feet.

Albert's brown horse was steady but it wasn't smart enough to do the driving. Longarm hurried back to the driving box long enough to grab the reins and pull the ambulance to a halt.

By the time he squeezed back through the pass-through, Nurse Hopkins was dead, her eyes staring sightlessly toward the ambulance ceiling, and Tom Ferris was lying strapped in his cot looking back at Longarm with clear, slightly fever-bright eyes.

There was complete awareness and a sharp intelligence in the eyes that the girl back at Fort Garland had told Longarm about in such glowing terms.

"Hello." Ferris smiled. His voice was scratchy with disuse but strong enough. "Would you mind telling me where I am and why I'm riding around trussed like a hog with a dead woman in the next bed?"

"I think this is gonna be a long story," Longarm said. "And I *sure* wish I had more answers for you than I do."

Chapter 32

They had covered Nurse Hopkins with a sheet from Tom Ferris's bed. Now Ferris was sitting up, giving all the appearances of being just fine, with one of Longarm's cheroots in his jaw and the last of Longarm's emergency travel rations of beef jerky and canned beans in his stomach.

"Damn, but I feel better now. Thanks. You, uh, wouldn't have a bottle of whiskey in that bag of yours, would you?"

"I do, but don't you think that'd be pushing it? I mean, you've been awful sick. Shouldn't you take it easy now?"

Ferris laughed. "I've been through this before, Long. Hell, maybe I'll go through it again a time or two before the consumption takes me."

"You seem easy enough about it," Longarm observed.

Ferris shrugged. "Nothing's gonna change it. I might as well be honest about it with myself and take what I can." He smiled. "An' a little drink of good liquor won't hurt at this point."

Longarm brought the bottle of rye out of his bag and handed it to his prisoner. Ferris had taken the news of his arrest quite as calmly as he did the disease that was slowly killing him.

"I earned it," he'd said. "I was pretty far gone with the laudanum, but I remember seeing those fellows. Funny thing, though. I don't remember hearing the gunshots when I burned them. I remember *doing* it, mind. I'm not denying that. I did it, and I'm sorry for it, but o' course being sorry won't bring them back. But what's odd, I remember seeing them and thinking that they were gunning for me for some reason, thought for that split second that I

163

was back in the war and they were Rebs, and of course I remember shooting them both. I can call t' mind the smell of the powder smoke just as clear as I can see you sitting there. But I can't remember ever hearing my gun go off. It's like it all happened in a dream and there was color and sight but no sound. Not a whisper of sound in anything I can remember." He'd shaken his head and told Longarm, "I won't give you any trouble, Marshal. I'm not a man who tries to deny what is." Then he'd smiled. "Besides, slow as the law works, I'll be dead of the consumption before I could live to meet the hangman."

Now Ferris took a long swig on the rye bottle, held the smooth liquor in his mouth for a moment, then swallowed with a sigh of contentment. "Ahhhh. That's nice."

He handed the bottle back, and Longarm took some himself before he returned it to his bag.

"You were saying about the things that've been going on since you found me at the hospital?" Ferris prompted.

Longarm filled him in on the rest of it. Tom Ferris was his prisoner, of course, as good as sentenced to hang despite the formalities of innocence until guilt is proven. Yet the man had been a good lawman in his time too.

Ferris nodded and wiped his mouth with the back of his hand. He started to say something but had to wait until a fit of coughing passed. When he could speak again he said, "I was there a little while, a few hours I guess I was, before I blacked out. I'd bet you they thought I saw something I oughtn't." His grin flashed again. "They were right, too. An' I'll bet you told 'em when you came for me that I'd been a law officer myself, didn't you?"

"I suppose I might have. What of it? And anyway, what could you have seen that anyone would object to?"

"Now that's what I know and you don't, isn't it. Tell you what, Longarm. I've heard about you. They say you're a straight shooter. And not just with a gun. I'll make a deal with you in swap for what I know about that situation down there and what you *need* to know."

"Ferris, you seem a likable enough fellow, but if you think . . ."

"No. No, dammit, it isn't that kinda deal that I'm proposing. Hell, you wouldn't go for letting me off and I wouldn't ask you to. I've already admitted to what I did in Trinidad. I'll stand up for it, and if the disease doesn't take me first I expect I'll swing for it. I can accept that. No, the deal I want is this.

"I have some pride, Long. One way or another, I've tried to give more to life than I've taken from it. I've served most of my adult life in the army, and I'm proud of that. I was a good officer. Then later I was a pretty damn good peace officer too, if I do say so. I gave it my best. After that, after I was using the opium so heavy that I couldn't be counted on except part of the time, I worked for old Otis Cornwall. But as a law enforcer, not a killer. I want you to know that, Long. I never once shot when I didn't have to." He grimaced. "Except that time in Trinidad, of course."

Longarm pulled out another cheroot and waited for the man to get the talking out.

"Anyway, the point is that I have my pride. I'm still a duly licensed peace officer with a special deputy's commission outa Alamosa County. I'd like to think, Longarm, that I can do one more decent thing before I go behind bars to pay for what I done. I'd like to go back and help you with something else—the something else that I know about an' you don't—before I'm locked away for the rest of my life." He grinned. "Not that that's so awful long to worry about, but still . . ."

"I can't . . ."

"It's pretty big, Long. And I hold the key to it. I'll give you my parole. My word as an officer and gentleman."

Longarm stared at him. Major Thomas Ferris actually *meant* it.

From most prisoners, a suggestion like that would be good for a hearty belly laugh maybe, but nothing else. But Tom Ferris truly meant what he said. He honestly wanted to go out on a note of duty rather than dishonor. And his word as an officer and a gentleman truly meant a great deal to him. Perhaps, Longarm realized, it meant *everything* to

165

him. It was all the dying man really had left.

Longarm pulled on his cheroot while he thought it over. Finally he said, "I'll go this far with you, Tom. I'll listen to what you have to say. Then I'll decide if we have a deal or not."

The suggestion was not as casually made as it sounded. If Tom Ferris was as genuinely interested in duty as he claimed—and Longarm was suspecting that he was—he would want his information known regardless of the personal consequences to him. If not, then the whole thing had been a scam and Longarm would drive on to Denver without looking back.

"All right," Ferris said without hesitation.

The thin consumptive smiled. "First thing, you're probably wondering what the hell brought me out of that coma, aren't you?"

"I damn sure am," Longarm admitted.

"Pull the plunger outa that syringe and smell of it. I can promise you you'll find strychnine in there."

"What the hell would that do?" But Longarm did as Ferris suggested. The unmistakable odor of strychnine was present inside the barrel of the syringe after Longarm removed the rubber-stoppered plunger.

"It's a quack remedy," Ferris explained, "though not the sort of thing a good doctor like Henscher would resort to. I've had it done to me twice by a barber-surgeon in Kansas when I was stationed at Fort Larned and was trying to keep the army from knowing how bad my disease had become. A consumptive, maybe other people too for all I'd know, but anyway a consumptive in a deep coma can sometimes be shocked out of it by a *small* application of injected strychnine. A little too much, of course, and there won't be any coming out of the coma. Which is why a proper doctor doesn't generally use the stuff. What the nurse there intended to give me, of course, was a deliberately fatal dose of the poison. What happened instead, I'd guess, is that a few drops of it got into me when she tried to inject me with the full dose."

"But why—?"

"I'm coming to that."

Longarm sat back and let the man continue at his own pace.

"I'm not a stupid man, Long. Just a sick one. And no one at the sanatorium knew I was a law officer when I checked in there. Not that I was trying to hide the fact from them. It's just that I was interested in looking for a cure for my disease and saw no reason to bring that up. And when I first got there I noticed several things that I would have brought to official attention on my own if I hadn't gone into that coma and if you hadn't come along so handily.

"I met Dr. Henscher, of course, and I have to say that I believe he is a fine, dedicated man. I believe that. But Dr. Henscher is only nominally in charge of things at the hospital that carries his name. I saw enough to realize that. I haven't any idea, frankly, who else is involved, but it was apparent that Henscher has his own staff of young college men while this other group has a virtually separate staff of young women."

Longarm raised an eyebrow.

"That's right. Quite separate. Oh, they seemed to get along well enough together. But the so-called nurses— they're nothing of the kind, by the by—were under the charge of that dead woman there, and the boys answering direct to Dr. Henscher."

"Those girls aren't nurses?'"

Ferris snorted. "Did you ever see one nurse in any group of ten that was pretty enough to want to bed? Of course not. Nurses look like that one." He pointed toward Hopkins. "Bunch of battle-axes, most of them. But the girls at the sanatorium are all pretty enough to make you drool."

Longarm had to admit that much.

"*One* o' the things this other bunch has going is a high-class whorehouse. Half the 'patients' staying at the hospital haven't any more consumption than you do. But they can check into the hospital with the full cooperation of their fat wives. They pay a hefty fee for the privilege, and they can have any nurse who walks in reach."

"How do you know all this? You were only aware of things for a matter of hours after you got there, you said."

Ferris grinned at him. "I met some of them on the porch, and of course they thought I was one of the phony patients just like them. They got to bragging about which of the girls they'd nailed and which other ones they figured to and how it was so dandy because their wives were all for them being there."

"I'll be damned," Longarm said.

"Must be a gold mine for Henscher's silent partners."

"Come to think of it," Longarm said, "Bertram did mention something about his family being poor and having to sacrifice so much to put him through school. I guess it just never connected with me how he could have been so poor to begin with and then come up with the money to build a facility like the sanatorium."

"That place cost a bundle to put up. You can just look at it and see that," Ferris agreed. "But hell, you just naturally think of doctors as having money. Nobody ever wonders how they came by it. It's like they're just naturally supposed to be rich. And of course they aren't. No more than anyone else. And research? There's no money in that at *all* until or unless the man succeeds with whatever wonderful discovery he's after. Until then it's all expense, not income. There isn't even time enough for a good researcher to have patients to pay his way."

"Never occurred to me to ask," Longarm admitted.

"It wouldn't have to me either," Ferris said. "But the whoring is only a part of what those boys, or girls, have going for them, Long. It's the third floor that's the big money-maker, I'll bet. And some of that I've seen."

"The third floor is the laboratory," Longarm said.

Ferris grinned. "Not but a piece of it," he said.

"I don't understand."

"You will. Look, I laid in that bed and I heard the footsteps and the partying above me."

"Partying?"

"That's right. Partying. *After* Dr. Henscher came down to make his rounds with the real patients like me. If I had

168

to guess I'd bet there isn't but a tiny little laboratory on that third floor. The rest of it is given over to guests that no one is supposed to know about being there. I heard them, Long. And by accident I happened to see some of them going past my room. I could hear them go up the stairs—which you may remember are damn well guarded day and night—and the partying after they got there."

"But who . . . ?"

"Outlaws," Ferris said grimly. "The doctor's partners are running a full-service hotel for men on the Wanted lists. I tell you, I saw several of them that I'm positive are on posters. One of them was a man name of Carlin. Harold Carlin. You know of him?"

Longarm nodded. Harold Carlin was wanted for a short, violent, and very successful series of train robberies several months back.

"I also saw a man I'm pretty sure is named Bartliss. Has a scar on him that you can't miss."

Damn. Longarm had mentioned being shot at. But he had not given Ferris any names. Ferris had seen Bartliss at the sanatorium just days before Bartliss tried to ambush and kill Longarm.

"Son of a bitch," Longarm said. "It makes sense. When I showed up looking for you, the men on the third floor would have thought I was a threat to them. That's why they wanted me grassed."

"I suppose so. And they wouldn't have known that I was a peace officer too. Or if they did, they might've figured I was playing possum and working with you instead of being the prisoner you claimed."

"One thing strikes me, though," Longarm said. "The simple, logical thing to do if they wanted to get rid of me would've been to just get rid of you. I mean, face it. You were there in that bed unconscious. Anyone could've walked in and pinched your nostrils shut. You'd have died, and no one would have thought a thing about it. Hell, you were expected to die."

"I don't think Dr. Henscher would allow anything like that. Like I told you, I still believe Henscher is every bit as

169

dedicated as he looks. He'd save a life if he could."

"I did notice one change," Longarm said. "When I first visited you in your room there was a nurse looking after you. Later it was a male attendant who was staying at your bedside."

"Makes sense to me," Ferris said. "Henscher wanted to preserve life. His partners wanted *both* of us dead to preserve their own skins. That would be why the nurse there came along and tried to kill me when you weren't looking. If you hadn't seen her make the try, everyone, you included, would have thought the trip was too much for me and I died of the consumption."

Longarm stood, having to duck to keep from bumping his head on the roof of the ambulance.

"Do you feel up to a drive back to the hospital?" he asked.

Ferris grinned. "This recovery period will only last a day or two. I'd sure like to help you while I can, Long."

Longarm crawled back onto the driving seat and made room for Ferris to join him.

He turned the gelding around and headed the ambulance back toward Monument.

Chapter 33

It was evening when they got back to Monument. Longarm made arrangements with Albert to have Nurse Hopkins's body taken care of, then he and Ferris went to the café so they could get a meal while they were waiting for Deputy Wisman to join them.

Ferris objected to bringing the locals in on the arrest.

"You and I can take them, Long. I'm sure we can."

"One, you and me probably *can't* take them if there's a bunch of them up on that third floor. Hell, we got no idea how many cases we're gonna clear with this one move. Second, *you* and me aren't taking anybody tonight. You're a *prisoner*, Tom. I can't give you a gun and holler 'sic em.' Billy Vail would have my butt for breakfast if I did a dumb thing like that. Furthermore, he'd be absolutely right to do it. So, I'm sorry, Tom, but you got to sit this one out. I'll give you full credit for the takedown. But I can't put a gun in your hands after I've already arrested you for murder. Be reasonable, man."

"I gave you my parole," Ferris complained.

"And I accepted it, Tom. You aren't in cuffs, and you won't be. You can come along and be a part of the raid. But there's limits, Tom. The idea of you carrying a gun and storming the trenches, that just wouldn't work. I'm sorry."

Ferris sighed, but he nodded. Then he smiled. "I'm becoming rather used to the idea of accepting the things I can't change."

"Good."

By the time they were finished with their supper, Buddy Wisman was there. Between them they filled the local deputy in on what they suspected they would find at the Henscher Sanatorium.

Wisman rolled his eyes and whistled. "Damn, Longarm. We've sure been proud of that hospital up there."

"As a hospital I reckon you still can be. It's only these other little details that need to be changed."

"How many men do you want?"

"Hell, how many can you give me? We have no idea what we're going to find. I think we should be ready to put half an army behind bars. That way if it turns out to be only a few guys, maybe a bunch of meek little embezzlers wearing sleeve garters, say, we're all right. The best arrests of all are the ones where the other guy throws his hands up and quits before anybody gets hurt, and the more strength we show the more likely that is to happen."

"All right. I can line up two dozen men if you like."

"Them and any others you can talk into it," Longarm said.

"I'll be back in a half hour," Wisman said.

"Don't forget transportation for everybody. It's a long walk. Trust me. I know."

Wisman smiled and left the restaurant.

"We have time for some pie," Longarm suggested.

"Good. I've missed a lot of meals I want to make up for," Ferris said.

Wisman was as good as his word. He was back in thirty minutes or less leading a ragtag group of townspeople who were carrying a wild assortment of arms. There was no drinking or rowdiness among them, though. Longarm was impressed.

"I've filled everybody in on what we're doing," Wisman reported, "and Albert is coming with enough wagons to haul everyone who isn't mounted."

"You've done mighty well," Longarm told him. "I'll make sure the sheriff knows about this."

Longarm stood on the seat of the ambulance and told the crowd, "Deputy Wisman has already told you what we have to do tonight. I want to add that we are not going up there to start a war. Anyone who wants to surrender peace-

172

ably is damn sure welcome to do it. Nobody shoots unless he has to, right? And remember, dammit, there are innocent people up there too. Playboys on vacation and genuine consumption patients. And we probably won't be all that interested in very many of the staff members either. Anybody working there will be taken into custody for questioning, but don't come down hard on them unless you have to. Most of them are likely innocent of any real wrongdoing. Any questions?"

"Just who the hell *are* we after if it ain't necessarily the staff," a man near the front asked.

Longarm had been thinking about exactly that all afternoon. He was not sure and wouldn't be until he had a chance to do some talking and some comparing of excuses and alibis, but he did have a guess.

"Probably a man who calls himself Donahue," he said. "He'll likely try to pass himself off as a salesman for hospital supplies. If you find that one, for damn sure don't let him go. Or anybody else you aren't sure of. It's easier to let them go later than try and catch them again after they've turned rabbit on you. To be on the safe side, you boys just worry about catching them. Deputy Wisman and I will be responsible for turning loose any we think are all right."

The man nodded and appeared to be satisfied.

"Then let's go do it."

The ride up the twisting, winding road onto Mount Herman seemed slower than ever before, and Longarm was acutely aware of the noise being made by three wagons and nearly a dozen saddle horses. Still, there was no getting around that. And no one would be expecting them at the hospital.

They reached the tent area first, and at Longarm's direction Wisman detailed half a dozen men to round up all the nurses and patients there and hold them for questioning.

"Most of these will be real consumptives and rich fellas coming to play with the nurses," Longarm explained. "The real trouble will be up at the hospital."

They halted the invasion force just short of the flat that

held the hospital building, and Longarm and Wisman counted noses among the remaining posse members. Since Wisman knew the men involved, Longarm let him handle the actual assignments, sending groups to sneak through the darkness and surround the long building on all sides.

Finally, when everyone had had time to get into position, Longarm turned to Tom Ferris.

"I'll expect to see you here when I get back, Tom."

"You have my parole, Long. My word of honor that I'll not try to get away. But I wish . . ."

"I can't, Tom. I just can't do that."

Ferris nodded.

"Ready, Buddy?"

Longarm, Wisman, and three hand-picked men would make the initial approach, right through the front door. With any degree of luck they could walk in, declare the place taken, and end it without a fuss.

"I wish we had a warrant to make this all legal," Wisman mused.

Longarm grinned and snapped his fingers. He reached into his coat pocket and pulled out a paper. "At your service, Deputy."

"What's this?"

"A warrant, of course. For party or parties unknown. I got it before we knew it was Ferris we needed for the Trinidad shootings, but we can fudge it in here."

Wisman looked genuinely relieved.

"I expect since you're the local law, Buddy, and there might be some question about jurisdiction, it would be better if you serve that paper on whoever's working Nurse Hopkins's desk tonight."

Longarm followed behind as Wisman and his three men crossed the gravel drive and mounted the steps onto the porch.

A handsome young attendant heard their footsteps and opened the door for them. The pretty blonde nurse Longarm had seen with Hopkins and Donahue before was behind the head nurse's desk.

"Good evening, miss." Wisman touched the brim of his

hat politely and showed the warrant to the girl.

"What's this?"

"I'm afraid everyone in this building is under arrest, miss. You will all be detained for questioning and then—"

"Raid!"

The pretty, innocent-looking girl shrieked the warning at the top of her voice and made a stab into a desk drawer for a nickel-plated revolver.

At least one of Buddy's hand-picked men had been damned well chosen. The man kicked the drawer shut on the girl's wrist, bringing a second yell out of her, this one filled with pain.

"You *broke* it."

"Could be," the man said calmly. He retrieved the revolver from the drawer and turned the girl so she was facing the wall. "Gee, Buddy, do I get t' check for other weapons?"

"Cocksucker," the girl hissed.

"No, but I hear you prob'ly do."

Footsteps thudded up the staircase, and a great many bewildered and almost certainly innocent people came wandering out into the hall to see what the hell was going on.

Longarm took off at a run for the stairs. A hand appeared over the banister on the second-floor landing. Lamplight gleamed on steel, and Longarm snapped a shot up the stairwell. The hand was withdrawn and the gun tumbled harmlessly down the stairs.

Longarm raced up to the second floor with Wisman and two of the deputies close behind.

A gun spat from the far end of the hall, and the man just behind Wisman was nailed in the temple just as his head cleared the level of the floor. He fell hard against the wall and slid back down, leaving a trail of blood behind.

Wisman and Longarm both returned the fire, and the man at the other end of the hall dropped. Longarm ran toward the man, noting that he was a civilian who was not wearing one of the hospital uniforms. A 'guest' from the third floor more than likely.

A door snapped open just as Longarm came near it, and his reflexes very nearly sent a slug into a white-haired, frail little woman who was looking out of her room to see what all the noise was about.

"Dammit, lady. Shut your door and get under your bed. Don't come out until somebody tells you it's okay."

The woman's eyes went wide and she bobbed her head vigorously before she scurried away to hide under her bed. She forgot to close her door, so Longarm did it for her.

By now Wisman was on the steps.

A hail of gunfire met him from above, and he staggered back down to the second floor with his left arm shattered and his teeth gritted.

"Shit," Wisman said.

"Yeah."

Longarm picked up a cushion from the chair the stair guard usually sat in and tossed it up the stairwell, toward the top floor.

Another volley of gunfire filled the building with sound, and splinters flew from the wooden stair-treads a few feet above the second-story flooring.

"They sure have this way covered. Is there another way up?"

Longarm couldn't believe that Buddy Wisman was still wanting to go forward. Most men would have quit with injuries half as serious as Buddy's arm looked.

"There isn't any that I know about," Longarm said.

By now there were sounds of a fight from outside too. The crash of shots and the tinkle of falling glass as windows in the building were targeted.

"Fire," someone above shouted.

There was no answering volley of gunshots, but soon Longarm could smell smoke curling down the stairwell. The gunfire from outside the building was still heavy but it had slackened markedly from the interior of the hospital.

"Somebody must have shot a lamp," Longarm said.

"I think we're fixing to have company."

Wisman and Longarm and the remaining deputy stood ready.

"Don't shoot," someone upstairs shouted. "We're coming down."

Longarm could hear the crackle of flames now as the wood of the building caught and the fire spread.

"Throw your guns down first."

There was a rattling on the stairs like steel hail as a variety of weapons was abandoned.

"Come down single file. Hands on your heads." Wisman took charge, and the third-floor guests came down one at a time. There were seven of them, and Longarm recognized all but two. Harold Carlin was among them, just as Ferris had said.

"That isn't everybody," Longarm said. "Where's Donahue? And for that matter where is Bertram Henscher?"

"The doc run for his laboratory when the fire started. Donahue run after him," one of the prisoners said.

"Take over here, Buddy. And make sure you get the innocents outa all these rooms."

"You can't go up there, Longarm!"

"I got to, Buddy. Bertram is stupid about who he takes in for partners, but I don't know that he's done anything exactly criminal. I want to bring him down."

"The place is going fast, Longarm."

Longarm looked at the man who had just spoken. He grinned. "Damn, Jimmy. I thought you were still in the pen."

"Naw. I got out a while back." Jimmy grinned back at his old adversary. "Good behavior."

"Well, keep your behavior good tonight, too. We'll talk over old times later."

Longarm started up the stairs at a run, leaving Wisman and his deputy to handle the evacuation.

Chapter 34

In just those few minutes the third floor of the Henscher Sanatorium had been turned into an inferno.

The smoke was thick, and active flames licked at the doors and walls on the entire west side of the building.

Streams of burning wallpaper curled and twisted. One fell across Longarm's shoulders, singeing him slightly until he could throw it off.

There was no sign of anyone alive on the top floor.

But Bertram had to be there somewhere.

The entire near end of the place was divided into small rooms, much like those on the floor below where the genuine patients were kept.

Longarm could hear shouting from down there now as people tired to flee the burning building, and the posse outside were still peppering the place with gunfire even though no one was shooting back at them any longer.

Surely the dumb bastards could see that the place was afire.

Longarm covered his nose with his handkerchief and ran down the hall.

Bertram's laboratory had to be at that end of the building.

He went to the last door he could see and tried to open it. It was locked.

This was no time to be polite. Nor to obey the doctor's instructions about do not disturb. A sign to that effect was nailed onto the laboratory door.

Longarm took a step back and kicked the door beside the lock.

Metal snapped and wood buckled, and the floor flew open.

"Oh, hell."

Jonathon Donahue was standing at an open window on the other side of a room filled with bottles and jars and gadgets that Longarm could not begin to comprehend.

The 'salesman' had a small-caliber Smith & Wesson in his hand, the muzzle of the nasty little weapon nestled in Bertram Henscher's right ear.

"A falling out of the partnership, Donahue?"

"One more step, Long, and I'll blow the good doctor's brains all over this lab."

"Then what?" Longarm asked reasonably. "The man can't protect you if he's dead. Wouldn't be anything then to stop me from putting a bullet into you, even if I had to shoot through him to do it. And this Colt would do exactly that."

"I won't be taken," Donahue insisted. "I'll shoot him first. I swear I will."

"Hell, if we don't all get out of here soon it won't matter who shoots who or not. We'll all be burnt to cinders anyhow."

"Back off, Long. You just back off a few steps and I'll leave you your doctor."

Longarm shrugged.

Hell, it seemed worth a try. It really did not matter if Donahue was alone in the lab or not if he would give up Bertram. The whole place was afire anyway, and there was nowhere he could run to.

"All right, Donahue. I'll go back into the hallway. Send Bertram out to me, and then it'll be just between us."

"Go on. I'll send him out."

Longarm nodded and warily edged backward.

The smoke in the hallway was thicker now, the flames more active. Another few minutes and there wouldn't be time for *any* of them to escape.

Donahue was up to something, of course. That only stood to reason. And Longarm had no real expectation of seeing Bertram Henscher walk out of the laboratory alone.

Longarm was amazed then when Bertram did just that.

Longarm had barely gotten out of the doorway before a badly frightened Henscher came running out of the lab with a rumpled mass of papers clutched in his arms.

"What the . . ."

"There's a fire escape, Longarm. Right out that window."

"Shit. Run for it, Bertram. You're on your own."

Longarm plunged back into the laboratory.

The room was empty now and the window open.

Longarm could hear Bertram coming behind him, apparently intending to take the fire escape rather than risk the flames in the hallway.

Fire was already covering the entire back wall of the hospital, licking hungrily at the iron fire escape ladder too.

There was no sign of Donahue. The man must have gone down the ladder like a monkey.

Longarm shoved the Colt into his holster so he would have both hands free and started down the ladder, Bertram following close behind him.

The metal of the ladder was hot as a poker from the live flames coming off the walls. Longarm had to grit his teeth and force himself to take handholds.

He glanced up toward Bertram. The doctor was having a rough time of it, trying to hang onto his laboratory notes and climb with one hand.

"Drop the papers, Bertram. We'll get them later."

Henscher started to say something. Then he let out a yell and jerked his hand off the ladder as the fire licked up the wall under his feet.

He lost his balance and fell, dropping hard on top of Longarm and carrying them both away.

The fall should not have been that hard, only a dozen feet or so, not all that much more than coming off a rank horse, but Bertram fell on top of Longarm and drove the breath out of him.

Henscher scrambled to his feet, grabbing for the papers that were being scattered by a fire-whipped breeze. Longarm was left on his back gulping for air.

"Thank you."

Longarm turned his head.

Donahue was crouched against the foundation of the building, the little revolver still in his hand and pointed now at Longarm's forehead.

Longarm's Colt was snug in his holster.

"You saved me the trouble of looking for you," Donahue said pleasantly. "After all, I believe you and the doctor there are the only ones capable of identifying me."

He smiled and thumbed back the hammer of the Smith.

Chapter 35

"Good-bye, Marshal."

Jonathon Donahue chuckled and raised his gun to take careful aim just above Longarm's eyes.

Longarm struggled to reach for his revolver. He knew he would be too late.

He would not lie there and take his death without at least trying.

A gun bellowed above him.

Yet there was no pain.

Longarm wondered about that. He really would have expected to feel a little pain when the end came.

Then he wondered what the hell he was doing all this wondering about. If he was still alive to be doing all this thinking . . .

He blinked and struggled to a sitting position.

Donahue was on the ground, the Smith unfired in his hand.

The shape of the man's head was distorted, his temples bulging outward from some unimaginable internal pressure, and his eyes and mouth popping.

A deep, wet depression had been gouged square on the top of his head.

Longarm looked up.

Tom Ferris was at the laboratory window Longarm and Henscher had just vacated.

Longarm could hardly see the former major, former lawman, for all the flame that was flooding the hospital building now.

He could see enough, though, to realize that Ferris was holding a Spencer carbine in his hands.

It must have been a heavy, .52-caliber slug from the Spencer that had dropped Donahue like a poleaxed shoat.

"Get down, man. Hurry."

The wood beneath the fire ladder supports was already burning away. Ferris could only have seconds left to make his escape.

"Tom. Hurry."

Longarm gulped in another breath, the intensity of the heat from the fire making it difficult to breathe even if he hadn't just had the wind knocked out of him.

"Hurry."

Major Ferris grinned at him and touched his forehead in a mocking salute.

"Better free than from behind bars, Long. And remember. I didn't run away. I gave you my parole."

"Tom. . . ."

But the windows was blank now, empty except for the glow of flames inside the laboratory.

Longarm scrambled to his feet and joined Henscher, who was staring up at the lab window also.

"All my dreams," Henscher said. "I could have done so much. I really could have."

"You still can, Bertram."

"I'll never be able to rebuild," he said.

"Somehow . . . some university or hospital."

Henscher sighed. "I'll go on trying, anyway."

Longarm took him by the arm and pulled him away from the building.

The entire thing was ablaze now, the night sky bright with it.

And Tom Ferris was somewhere inside the furnace that had been a hospital.

Slowly the roof began to buckle at the far end of the building as the supports were burned away.

"Come on, Bertram. This is too close to be safe."

Longarm thought he could see tears in the tough rugby player's eyes as he pulled the doctor to safety.

Longarm listened very closely, but there was no final scream of agony from Tom Ferris.

The man died with as much dignity as he had lived for most of his life.

Longarm thought Ferris would have been proud of that.

And Longarm intended to make very sure that Major Thomas Ferris received full credit for breaking up Donahue's scheme.

That would be the least, and the last, Longarm could do for a brave and honorable man who had made just one fatal mistake.

"Come on, Bertram," Longarm said. "You've got a *lot* of talking to do to me and a county deputy named Wisman."

Henscher nodded numbly and trudged at Longarm's side as they made their way around the collapsing hospital building to join the crowd out front. A wall caved in, sending a spray of burning embers into the sky in a column that would be visible for many miles.

Longarm watched a bright glowing spark rise on the superheated currents of air as the last of the roof fell in. He could not help wondering if Tom Ferris's spirit was rising with the starlike sparks toward a peace the man had not known here.

Watch for

LONGARM AND THE BLOOD BOUNTY

one hundred sixteenth novel in the bold
LONGARM series from Jove

coming in August!